fireWife

Nan A. Talese

Doubleday

New York   London   Toronto

Sydney   Auckland

fireWife

TINLING CHOONG

APR 0 2 2007

PUBLISHED BY NAN A. TALESE

AN IMPRINT OF DOUBLEDAY

Copyright © 2007 by Tinling Choong

All Rights Reserved

Published in the United States by Nan A. Talese, an imprint of The Doubleday Broadway

Publishing Group, a division of Random House, Inc., New York.

www.nanatalese.com

DOUBLEDAY is a registered trademark of Random House, Inc.

Three chapters of this book have appeared, in different form, in the following publications:

"I Am Bangkok Ut" in *The Sun*, "Maria and Fire Breast" in *The Minnesota Review*, and "Wing

Joyce is winged" (under the title "Lip") in *The Literary Review*.

Book design by Maria Carella

Library of Congress Cataloging-in-Publication Data

Choong, Tinling.

FireWife/Tinling Choong.—1st ed.

p.   cm.

I. Women photographers—Fiction.   2. Asian American women—Fiction.   3. Identity

(Psychology)—Fiction.   I. Title.

PS3603.H665F57 2007

813'.6—dc22   2006044566

ISBN-13: 978-0-385-51645-7

ISBN: 0-385-51645-2

PRINTED IN THE UNITED STATES OF AMERICA

1 3 5 7 9 10 8 6 4 2

First Edition

Foremost, I dedicate this small book to my baby daughter
For when she is a woman and embarks to discover her self and place
In the big scheme of yin/yang, fact/fancy, known/unknown, fire/water, chaos/order
May Buddha bless her with a life
Long, strong, good, full of love, friends, humor, insight, and guiltless delight

I also dedicate this book to:
My mother, who loves her children more than herself
My father, who loves his children quietly and totally
My husband, who is my bay of the sea
My three brothers, who make me laugh

death

in between lives

life

prologue, misplaced

THIS IS THE STORY OF EIGHT WOMEN,
four fire and four water, bonded since the genesis—
when Nuwa pushed open the egg of time.

THEY ARE:

Lakshmi: previously known as *Fire*

Nin: *Vessel*

Zimi: *Egg*

Ut: *Innocent*

Table: *Stable*

Wing: *Mirror*

Maria: *Mother*

Milk: *Water*

Zoom in

You'll see the eight women in their present incarnations

See their now tenuous bonds continue on

Despite the fragmentation in our time

See the women cross paths

Fleetingly

Not knowing their ancient bonds

Barely fulfilling their ancient destinies

See their stories intertwine

Over the Body and Mind of Time

Organically yet not too organically

Accidentally yet not too accidentally

Bind

Unbind

Bind

Life

Death

Life

death

In Genesis, Fire was fated to fan hot the seed
in between Vessel's legs so that Vessel can fly . . .
Vessel was made to crave the touch of bliss, of flight,
of blissful flight . . .
THE MYTH

chapter 1

LAKSHMI: *Fire*

*P*arvati, please don't be afraid. I won't harm you. I'm Lakshmi, daughter of Sita. Remember Sita, my ma? Sita, your oldest sister who could hand loom the finest khadi in India? Yes, Sita. I'm Sita's daughter. I'm Sita's only daughter. Yes, I'm your niece. I mean, I was your niece. I'm glad you remember, Parvati. I'm happy to meet you finally. I'm Lakshmi. I mean, I was Lakshmi. We never met. I hope I don't frighten you talking to you in your dream.

Parvati, your brows are black horse-mane brushes, just as I've imagined, just like Ma's. May I sit down on the slope between your brows? I've run so many dream-miles in six days. My legs are screaming. It feels so good to sit down. I think better when I sit down, too. And I need to think better because I'm here to plant a dream that has a root cotton-thread long and intertwined. I'm also here to make a small request. Please stay asleep and hear me speak.

You know, Parvati, Ma talked about you often. Your bold charcoal eye liners, your strong coconut-oiled hair, your enormous second toes, your nine-inch palms, your cypress arms, your heavily ornate nose, your famous spit into what's-his-name's face, your going to secretarial school in Bombay, your brown hat fat cigar photograph, your wild love with a snake charmer despite his cobras, your rearing of a mongoose later, your first cigarette in the closet, your forgetting-own-stomach type of giving, your fire-speed wit, your straight face humor, your dreaming of a white elephant with wings, your marrying a Chinese man, your improvised golden red sari that fitted like pants, your diligent reading of western magazines under moonlight, your meal-forgetting learning of the English language, your confidence, your independence, your freedom, your strength were my childhood stories.

Parvati, so many times I imagined you a winged white elephant with forty-four pure gold nose rings. Other times, I thought you a sacred cow with one five-pound gold hoop looped around both your nostrils. Secretly, Ma and I thought of you for strength. You were inside us. You were the venom, the power, the dream.

Ma said I was like you, Parvati. I'm still like you. I long for wild love. No offense to Pa and Ma, softdeeplong kind of love bores me. Neither am I equipped to love softlydeeply-longly. I'm afraid if I'm in such a love I may accidentally yawn making love or snore out loud in the middle of his medium-spicy orgasm. And I may get so bored that my female mustache may start growing itself denser and stiffer under my nose.

Like you, Parvati, I long for wild fire love. The kind that goes amok across the Himalayas, over the Deccan plateau. The kind that boils dry all the water in the Bay of Bengal and the Arabian Sea. The kind that drove you to walk ten miles to borrow books and learn to read. The kind that consumed you and the snake charmer. And like you, I feel my tiger all the time. My lips are hungry. All the time. Fire leaps in my jugular. All the time. I am hungry. I am ready. Ready to walk-talkreadwritethinklaughfightlove in a fire storm way.

But Ma said wild love doesn't last. She said there is no such thing as a sustainable wild love or a committed passion. None. Ma said passion is passion only if it is spontaneous and momentary. A constant ecstasy is no ecstasy. A long passion is no passion. Since big happiness comes with big sorrows, big love grows big hatred; she said water love is better than fire love. The best is three parts water and one part fire. But she said knowing me, Sita's daughter, the most water I can garner is probably one part. So I should be realistic and strive for one part water and three parts fire instead.

She knew, like you, I am all four parts fire. And I am a tiger.

But Ma said that I must make peace with my fire tiger inside. I must learn to tame her. And if I tame her well, then occasionally, I can choose to let her loose, go amok, fight for truth, make fire, make love. Only then will I have a satisfied face in my next life.

But here I am, in between lives, and my face is far from satisfied. I should have listened to Ma. I should have tamed my fire tiger so that her eyes could see far and clear. I should have fed my tiger at least one part water.

Parvati, I hope I don't frighten you. I'm a ghost now. I became a ghost six days ago. Please stay in dream while I tell you my death, my journey, my life.

I married the youngest son of a textile distributor a year ago. That was two years after Ma died in her dream. Poor Pa wanted to give me all his three wooden hand looms as dowry. I couldn't. I took only one. But, deep in our hearts, Pa and I knew one or three looms, they were meager without distinction. Pa was worried about me being bullied because of the small dowry. I hugged Pa and told him Vasu loves me, he despises the caste system, he will protect me. And I used my small savings and bought myself a gold nose ring and Pa a new pair of convex glasses.

The day I married, Pa's sallow eyes were old wells choked with water and love. Later, Pa spent all his time waiting for the wheel of reincarnation to come. He prayed to elephant-headed Ganesha. Mornings. He prayed to Rama.

Nights. He asked Rama and Ganesha if he could join Ma in next life. Pa died two months after I married, in his dream. Truly, their love is Ganges, flowing deep and long. Defying place. Defying time.

Like you, Parvati, when I married, I was hungry and ready to die for anything passionate—a spiritual love, a sexual love, an ultimate truth, a social justice, or a cause to alleviate any human suffering. I was sixteen. My tiger was blissfully drunk. Drunk swimming in a lake of flaming love wine. I sincerely thought I found a half human half divine, a two-parts-water-two-parts-fire man. Yes, I do I do I do, I said, I love you, Vasu.

But, Parvati, my tiger was fierce but blind. I married a man far from human, let alone divine. I married a serpent husband. Incidentally, I also married the other thirty-four snakes in his family.

You see, Parvati, he spoke all the right words. His mind was as sexy as his body as his scent as his words. I thought he was different. He told me he didn't care that I was a shudra and that I was poor. He told me he would teach me to read and write and he would buy all the books I wanted and I could read till I died. He told me it didn't matter whether I was a shudra or a vaishya. He told me he needed me. He told me he would protect me from all harm. He told me he wanted me to be the mother of his child. He told me it was his dharma to love me. He told me I was the most precious in his life. He told me he remembered buying a lotus flower from me in our previous lives. He told me he would stand up for me if his parents, sisters, brothers looked down on me.

Those vaishya snakes. Not all vaishyas I knew were snakes. But those were. Parvati, I married a pantheon of snakes. Smiling snakes. Drooling snakes. Filial snakes. Indifferent snakes. Biting snakes. Pregnant snakes. Fashionable snakes. Khadi-wearing snakes. Wrapped in gold bangles snakes. And then there was this greedy father-in-law python who would swallow an elephant whole and worry about digestion problems later. I sincerely did not notice their blood was cold like the freezer in a refrigerator. I married indeed a pantheon of icy fangs and big bellies. Bite, kill, tear, swallow, digest, breathe. Bite, kill, tear, swallow, digest, breathe. That's what snakes do best.

The fact is that Vasu had neither fire nor water in him. Only intelligent cowardice and a lot of snake shits. I believe he *was* in love with me. For half a year or so. That was before we were married. You see, Parvati, he was the youngest in the family and therefore had the least power. He married me because his parents were old and they wanted their remaining unmarried child to fulfill his dharma as a son. He married me because the family needed a pair of cypress arms to boil, cook, wash, sweep, clean. He married me because I had nice face nice body and he wanted to share a bed with me. He married me because I was aflame with love and he was no fool. He married me because I was a shudra and shudras are good serfs and shudras don't complain much.

Well, too bad. This shudra complained. And this shudra fought like a warrior. With twenty fingers forty toes. Just to survive all sorts of snake bites. But their blood was still freezer cold. When I spoke up, dirty snake underwear doubled in piles waiting for me to wash. Hate in snake eyes grew eight-fold in size. Beatings became twice a day.

One time the dowry matter came up. The father-in-law python punched his mad hammer fist onto my face and tore my gold nose ring off and said it's time to get rid of me for a new wife a bigger dowry. As if he needed more rupees to secure an additional layer to his python-belly fat. And I was supposed to revere this man, the almighty father-in-law. Where were our scores of Gods and Goddesses? I bled. I bled because my gold nose ring was stolen. The nose ring was you, Parvati. You were my strength. I sat you on my nose. And he tore you off. I ran to the police. The police looked at my bleeding nose and black eye and asked what I did wrong.

The truth is that I was a girl and a shudra. I was a sub-class. A less-than-a-slave slave. Really, they respected cows and fish more than they did me. They didn't kill cows. And they ate fish with care. I think they felt that they had made a rotten deal. Because this sub-serf—I—took their words bravely. Kneaded them into steel arrows and shot them back quickly. And I had good eyes and aimed well.

My tiger was completely sober when Vasu slapped me, for the first time. I spat on his face hard hoping to pierce a hole on his cheek through the back of his head. But I missed. I spat on his ear instead.

And all this while, I was hoping Garuda would stop by. You know Lord Vishnu's mount? The white-faced bird? The one with the body and arms of a person, feet, beak, and wings of an eagle. The one who carries Lord Vishnu on her golden back. I prayed. Mornings and nights. I prayed for Garuda because I heard she's an excellent serpent devourer. I was hoping she would stop by and have a big dinner.

Those vaishya snakes. The day Vasu told me it's my duty to obey and endure, that was it. I told him it's my dharma to see him and all his snake-blooded relatives nailed on a needle bed and skinned alive and bled to death or their skin burned or their flesh eaten by dogs. He whacked my head with the ten-pound holy book in his hand and asked how could I, a serf, forget my place and have blood this bad. Whacked. I said you bloody son of a bastard snake. I spat on his face right into his left nostril. That was a real hot joy.

By then, my hope had wilted to zero. It was only six months ago that my tiger was swimming drunk in his mouth on his bed the first time. Amazing how fast things could change. I packed up all my papers into a handkerchief. I carried them with me in my secret pocket inside my sari. I was all ready to go to Bombay. I was going to Bombay to learn to read. I was ready to pluck chickens or sell lentils or dry tea leaves or work as a tailor assistant to save up all the rupees I needed to learn to read so that I could become a teacher, a librarian, or a letter-writer. I had heard that a tailor assistant could make thirty rupees a day in Bombay.

Then no blood came that month. My heart almost fell off my tongue. Garuda didn't stop by. A new life did instead.

Parvati, I didn't know I wanted a baby so bad. I forgot about the rupee-saving handkerchief I hid in my sari. The snake underwear pile shrunk in front of me. I knew they were waiting for a baby with a man thing. I didn't care about their subtle caring. My tiger grew very happy. I wanted my baby. I told them I'm keeping the baby. Boy or girl. I told them I'm keeping the baby even if sky collapses, sun perishes, moon breaks, rivers die, I want my baby. I told them I'll scorch them alive if they scratch even one baby fingernail.

I wondered why Garuda did not stop by. The fourth full moon after I became pregnant, Vasu's father and two brothers tied me up and drove me to some back-street sonography clinic. My belly was scanned. It was said to contain a disappointing vagina. Just as they had suspected. With force they ordered apart the mouth between my legs. Further and further. I squirmed. I kicked. I boxed. I cursed all Gods. My every tooth-root split into halves. Earth was sucked out. She was red, puce, wet, and really pretty. She had a broad smile. So broad that I could not help thinking she must feel so lucky not having been born to me, her ma, whose eyes were swollen black grapes, whose back had scars like a nest of centipedes. Her broad smile hurt me. Bad.

Parvati, I can't tell you what followed because I don't know. I don't remember. For weeks, I could feel nothing. I must have been an afternoon shadow for weeks. No pain. No joy. No moon. No sun. No sky. No Ganges. No Gods. No snakes. No nose ring. No dreams. Really, for weeks, an oil bottle or his thing, I couldn't tell the difference. For weeks, my tiger was hibernating, deep in earth, deep in my navel.

Ironically, it was a smiling snake, Vasu's number four brother, who brought back flesh and blood to my shadow. I had always known that he drooled in his pants when I was around. He came so close to doing his snake himself in front of me in the kitchen once. I tried to splash a ladle full of hot ghee at his body. He slapped me with the back of his hand, and said you idiot you think I do this to anyone, this is a compliment to you, you pig brain. Slapped. So I told him to take his snake and do it in hell. Splashed.

Parvati, I don't care whether none or few or many drool in their pants when I walk by. You see, like you, I think sexual fantasies are the bones of life. Beautiful indeed. But I kept my drooling in my panties. I kept my drooling quiet. I never saw my drooling as compliments and that the handsome fishmonger or the friendly cobbler or the curry powder shop owner or the rickshaw cycler was to say "thank you for drooling in your panties, madam," "thank you for wanting to touch me, madam," "thank you for your wet desire seeing my face my body, madam." And I would never never think of taking that small step beyond and dancing my tongue in front of them or forcing them to poke their snakes into me by waving a cleaver.

But nonononono. Vasu's number four brother had to sit on me. Deep. He had to murmur into my ear while waving a small kitchen knife, "you're lucky because I like you," "your panties are soft I want to come inside you," "your breasts look sweet I want to squeeze."

Flesh and blood rushed back to my shadow to my rescue. So I bit a half piece off his crispy left ear. His blood was surprisingly sweet. As he screamed and scrambled, my tiger leaped high into the air. For the first time in weeks.

Moments later, I was boiling water in the kitchen, thinking of my lost and found power and tiger and fire and Bombay. Three brothers and two wives and the God-like father-in-law python snaked into the kitchen and poured kerosene onto my long hair. They lit a match. Snake's wife shrieked how dare I seduce her husband. Others spat and yelled, "filthy worthless evil woman go back to hell."

You know, Parvati, I had dreamed of a violent fire bed four nights before I died. And for the next four days, I had suffered from a kerosene nose attack. The nose just came. Coated in kerosene. I could smell nothing. Except for the kerosene. Kerosene left. Kerosene right. Kerosene up. Kerosene down. Kerosene in and out my nose. The omen came and lingered for four days before I died. But I didn't pay attention to the omen. I was a shadow then. I was so light, so hollow. I could feel so little. I offered neither curiosity nor resistance to the omen. I thought briefly a friendly ghost was doing its prank. You know how they like to pinch and you wake up with green bruises on your thighs. Or kiss you a hickey on the chest. Silly things like these. Really, I could not have cared less.

Until they poured kerosene onto my long hair. And lit a match. And threw it onto my nose. My kerosene nose took it and exploded. Those vaishya snakes.

I opened my mouth. My tongue was on fire. I squirmed. I extended my fire arms. I ordered them to look straight into my fire eyes and remember well. I know they did, Parvati. All of them suffered from a sudden rapid diarrhea in their pants as I walked toward them in my fire sari and spoke with my fire mouth in my fire voice. I walked on my fire feet from the kitchen through the dining room to the living room and sat on the python's high-back power-chair. A fire tiger flew out my mouth, see you guys around, I squirmed. And I let out a strong string of ghostly laughs. They cowered with pee-shit rushing between their legs. Their legs cemented. That was a real hot joy. Indeed.

. . .

Parvati, do you remember the story of how Prince Rama rescued his wife Sita from Ravana's hideaway? How Rama loved Sita so deeply but was bound by sacred law and could not take her back because she had lived under another man's roof during her captivity? And how Sita fulfilled her dharma by jumping into a funeral pyre? And how Fire God Agni refused to take her and she walked back out of the fire unscathed and her name was cleansed and Rama was allowed to take her back?

Moments after I completely left my body, Fire God Agni arrived. He told me to go back! He said that I deserved the right to live and prove the purity of my name. I couldn't believe my ears. What's wrong with this Guy? What's there to prove? I told him, I, with all due respect, happily forfeit my right. I swore I would rather have my tongue cut and my fingers crushed than to live among those snakes again. Take a good look at their hearts, I politely asked. He right away understood. He knew! Parvati. He knew that even if I went back they would pour more kerosene onto my body and sear me fiercer. He knew the seed of malignity and murder had bloomed in the snakes' hearts.

So, Fire God Agni took me. And I found out that I was not alone. There had been hundreds of girls and women who had rejected Fire God Agni's offers to revive them and cleanse their names and heal their wounds burned in by funeral pyres and dowry-related fire murders. His kind intention to purify our names shocked me. Parvati, I didn't know Goddesses and Gods could be so out of touch with worldly reality. I thought they must have at least heard of the famous Punjabi proverb that says: the luckless man is the one who loses a horse; the lucky man is the one who loses a wife. I thought they were the almighty and they must know how difficultly some of us lived.

Then I was told about the Book of Karma. I was also told that I, like other good intermission-ghosts, was bestowed six days to rest my panting soul-lungs. I could do anything I wanted during the six days. Anything non-evil of course. And I was told a little mischief wouldn't affect my karma status. That was good to know. Because I was planning on going back to set a small fire on the python's graying nose hair. I was willing to cash in some of my karma just to make him cower and pee in his pants one more time. In fact, I would have cashed in all my karma just for that.

But I spent the morning of my first day head-buried in the Book of Karma. Finally, on page 8,136,868,998, Volume VIII, I spotted Pa's and Ma's names and faces. Ma had most recently forgone her destiny to be born into comfort and had chosen to become a tree at the shoulder of Ganges. So had Pa. I ran to see them right away. Trees are rare in the Holy City of Varanasi. Pa and Ma were giving shade to a group of pilgrims from Madras who had just finished taking their holy bath. Parvati, their love is Ganges, so good, so deep, so long. Can you believe that Pa's and Ma's love has flowed for nine lifetimes now? According to the Book of Karma, Pa and Ma first met in 1499. That was a year after the Portuguese traveler Vasco da Gama landed at Calicut seeking spices. Pa was a well-traveled compass maker from China, and Ma the third daughter of a famous Indian thread seller.

We hugged. We talked. And talked. For a longlonglong time. I told Ma I wanted to become a tree next to them. I told her I've had enough of the human world. And I wanted to do what they did—to forgo what my karma had accumulated—my fate to be born into love and comfort in my next life. Parvati, I was determined to become a tree next to Ma and Pa. Loved and loving, safe and shade-giving, and serene.

But Ma looked deep into my eyes and said Lakshmi, you are four parts fire. You are a tiger. Water love doesn't suit you. Being a tree means you partake in life differently. Often you can only observe life from afar. Tree love does not suit you, Lakshmi. You must go and find out what you want to do with your next life. You have accumulated good karma. You have now a chance to be born free, to fight for truth, make fire, make love. Go see the world. Go walk the earth. Go fly the air, swim the water, taste the dew. Tame your tiger and fire well. Go find your water. Go. But do not revenge. The hands of Karma will take care of things fairly. Do come back and tell us what you learn and what you decide. Pa and Ma will always be here. We love you very very much. Go. And remember to always see wide and deep.

And remember, Lakshmi, *when you break a fruit of a banyan tree you see very tiny seeds and when you break a seed you see nothing in it and what you do not see is the essence of the banyan tree.*

Go, Lakshmi.

Embracing Ma's advice, I left Ganges and ran southwest.

Bombay was bleeding bad, Parvati. I saw forty women go into the back-street ultrasonic clinics in a morning. Six baby-earths were sucked out. Lifeless. Six! Parvati. Six. They were puce, wet, and very pretty. Each of them had a vagina and a broad smile. Six small earths died in one Bombay morning. Six in a city of eighteen million is six too many. Then I saw a woman waking up in her fire bed and her kerosene nose exploded. Big. She was set aflame and burned to death and she begged Fire God Agni not to send her back. And I saw how her house-snakes bribed policemen without a pea bit of guilt and shame on their faces, they claimed a stove fire started the accident, they said she was always clumsy with the pots and pans anyway.

Oh, Parvati.

By then, all my anger my tears had transmuted into a fire tiger. Running. Screaming. Seeing. Penetrating lives of girls and women on fire. Trying to make sense.

Taking Ma's advice, I turned to lands beyond India.

Fire tiger flew fiercer and fiercer, flying east south north west, waywardly, up, down, left, right . . .

Until . . .

Until I met Nin . . . and the women she photographed.

As I sensed and made sense through Nin's skin and the women's skins, a loosening of truth occurred—the truth of women of fire and women of water. The Truth emerged at the end, where I thought I saw a flickering, empty of everything and also nothing, sitting there like a queen. A woman. A vessel complete.

Parvati, please stay asleep while I share with you the lives of the women I met in my journey. Please stay in dream while I tell you the emotions and memories amassed in the moments I penetrated, saw, felt, and lived.

chapter 2

NIN: *Vessel*

e were at Good-Grandma's Tapioca House that afternoon. December 31, 1981.

We called Mama's mother Good-Grandma because she was fun and kind. Good-Grandma's house was adjoined to the tapioca factory which she had run single-handedly since Good-Grandpa was killed during The Emergency by a British soldier who mistook him for a notorious communist. It's said that Good-Grandpa and the notorious communist shared these common characteristics: they were bald in the head and short in build and Chinese. Good-Grandpa was shot in the stomach in late 1955 but didn't die until August 31, 1956— exactly a year before Malaysia got her independence from the British Empire.

That afternoon, the dog, Come-Luck, breath as pungent as the bibulous coolie in charge of stirring muddy liquid tapioca at the field of open tapioca wells, was barking at a group of sparrows about to spread their wings through the fresh-washed sky.

"Mian! The rain has stopped! Let's play *Lost in Space!*" I hollered.

I was seven years old, and Mian five.

"Yippi dubba doooooooo!!!" Mian was instantly her perky self again.

"Good-Grandma's pillow, we can make it our door, and the fluffy ones mark our spaceship, and the area within is the command post and the place we eat and sleep. And, Mian, this time, you are the big brother, okay, Mian?"

"But, Jie, I am younger. And also, I am a girl. Can I be big and brother?"

Silly Mian, forever full of questions, my small sister, I love her.

And I love the nasal way she called me Jie—elder sister.

"Of course, you can!" I said. "Jie doesn't want to be the responsible and eldest one again. I am already the eldest one. I am never going to be smaller like you or smallest like Liang." My brother, Liang, was standing nearby sucking his thumb. "So, Mian, you have to pretend you are big and brother at least for one time. Okay? Plus, today is my birthday, I don't want to be your responsible big sister today."

"Can I be big and brother at the same time, Nin?" When unsure, Mian always frowned her cute frown, which involved not only her brows but also the top of her nose. And every now and then she called me by my name.

"Of course, you can be big and brother at the same time," I persuaded her in pure confidence. "Like this, you keep your eyes open but don't look at anything. Make yourself loose and soft. Then think you are big and brother and brave and you can kill the Monster Centipede. If you think it, it is real. Trust Jie. It can be as real as this hibiscus bush, this bench, these pillows. Plus, you get to drive the space-scooter, get off the space-scooter, and kill the Monster Centipede on MonkeyMud Planet. Okay, Mian? Just this time, let Jie be the small one. Let Jie be the small sister who does whatever she likes. And you be the big one in charge of fighting Monster Centipede. Okay, Mian?"

"Okay, Jie! Look at my sword, Jie. My sword is as long as my long spoon."

"And, Mian, remember the joke I told you about how Centipede Mama went broke buying shoes for her Centipede Babies?"

Mian chuckled. "And the Earthworm Mama went bank-rupt buying belts for her children. Oh yaaaa, I am the big sister . . . I mean, big brother. I'll kill many centipedes and a thousand pairs of shoes will cover MonkeyMud Planet! Yippi! I will protect you and Liang from centipedes' long tongues. I see what you mean, Jie, I am soft and loose. My scooter is shaking. Jie, do centipedes have birthdays? Do they celebrate birthdays like we do?"

"Yes, they do!" I said. Looking at the Casio watch I just got for my birthday, I announced, "Let's start playing *Lost in Space* in two minutes, at three p.m. sharp!"

"Jie, do centipedes have tongues?"

"I don't know, Mian. You are in charge of finding that out. Okay, Mian?"

"Okay. Roger. Over."

"Over, Mian. Let's see . . . the red fluffy pillow is the pilot seat . . . but we have no Doctor Smith. That's okay. We have the Robot. Liang, you be the Robot in *Lost in Space*. A small robot big enough to say warning warning w a r n i n g danger danger danger d a n g e r. Can you do that, Liang?"

"w a i n g . . . l a n j e r."

Liang was born with a slow tongue, my Other-Grandma constantly reminded us. We called Pa's mother Other-Grandma because, unlike our Good-Grandma, Other-Grandma had a presence menacing as a Godzilla. And because Pa was a filial son, growing up, we lived with the Godzilla in her Kinta House in the tin-rich town of Kinta. To my Other-Grandma's frequent reminder of Liang's slow tongue, Mama rebutted that Liang would one day prove the whole world wrong, he would become the greatest lawyer with the quickest tongue. Like Mama, I thought Liang was just taking his time. I knew he was smart. People didn't understand because he always agreed. I wished he would ask more questions. When you ask questions, people think you are smart.

"Very good, Liang. Also, swing your arms like this when you say warning warning danger. Say it only when Jie gives you the brow-look, okay, Liang?" Churning my arms like fans, I turned my brows into a sleeping S.

Nodding, Liang pointed at Mian and said, "Jie, look! Jie . . ." I turned to look at Mian.

"Mian, why are you running crooked and making your eyes cocked?" I asked.

"I am big and brave and brother, that's why one," Mian answered, running like Jackie Chan's Drunken Master. "And my space-scooter is shaking, that's why two!!" she yelled back. Her voice was happy pinkpink happy. Clad in her favorite pink dress, waving her long spoon, Mian ran about in the field of open tapioca wells not far from our pillowed spaceship parked on the bench by the hibiscus shrub.

Mian died that day. December 31, 1981.

I was seven years old, a tiger, and she five, a dragon.

December 31, 1981. My birthday. Mian's deathday.

A Thursday.

They found Mian at 4 p.m.

4 p.m. Mian's death time.

A fiercely pink hero, brave and big and brother, Mian ran after the centipedes into the deepest tapioca mud well and drowned, while I, the *real*-big-but-*real*-small-want-to-be, stayed within touch of the soothing skin of five fluffy pillows, busy preparing fake mango curry and fake papaya ice cream in half coconut shells. Whereas Liang was the small robot BIG enough to utter, without the urge of the sleeping-S-brow-look from his big sister, in toothless voice: l a n j e r l a n j e r LAN J e r LAN J e r LANJER DANJER DANGER!!!!!!! He swung his small arms like two electric fans.

I did not hear him that day.

I was smaller than he was and carefree, you see.

I was also guilty.

No one saw but I was the killer.

No centipedes, no slippery tapioca well, no running-nose sky could make me free.

No excuse could free me. No.

I refused to be freed.

I made Mian cock-eyed.

I made her big when she was only five, and she died.

Forgive me.

Punish me. I said repeatedly.

This guilt crawled low in my blood.

It still does.

It erects my hair like trees whenever it wants to.

It can only die when I die.

December 31, 1981. 4 p.m. I imprisoned the small and bad and carefree and careless Me voluntarily, quietly, maturely, like any big sister would do for a small sister who died saving her big sister and small brother from Monster Centipede.

December 31, 1981. We were at Good-Grandma's Tapi-oca House in the village of Terong that afternoon because my Other-Grandma, the Godzilla, had thrown Mama's clothes from inside Kinta House onto the main street of Kinta at 12 p.m. sharp. Mian, Liang, and I were playing *Lost in Space* on the Kinta main street pavement at that exact moment. The last day of the year, school ended earlier than usual. All the Kinta town folks and children were home early. Like us, they saw Mama's clothes shooting into the street, propelled and sus-tained for an unusually long time in the noon air by the sim-ple rage of my Other-Grandma. She was a tiger.

I asked Mama once if I could change to be a rabbit like her or a dragon like Mian or a horse like Liang. Mama ex-plained that tiger has many kinds. You can be a good one. She didn't say you are a good one. She said I can be a good one.

Can Be is dangerous and can be bad.

Underneath Mama's airborne clothes, I saw the neigh-bors' eyes piercing from the deep shadows in their living rooms through the gaps in their front doors. The eyes had teeth. Sharp ones. I saw the gaps of their front doors turn into the gaps of their front teeth, out of which gossip would self-sprout and self-feed.

Mama left her clothes untouched on the main street that

day. We left our chalk-drawn spaceship sitting apologetically on the sidewalk. We made a line walking down the main street heading toward Good-Grandma's Tapioca House in the next village, fifty stone-throws from Kinta House. Kinta people's eyes had teeth. They nibbled at my feet. A blind-white noon. Windless and peopleless, the street smelled faintly of smoked rubber, and stray dogs stood like amputees. Hissing crickets hissed us along. I wished we were on horses, like the cowboys with long chins in *Bonanza*, vanishing into the end of their Main Street, into sunset, into justice, into a happy The End. But we walked. Slowly. Mian's hand and my hand fastened like Elephant Glue. Liang sucked his thumb in Mama's arms. Walking down Main Street that day, I was glad Mama left her clothes behind this time, and I was also glad she did not cry like last time.

In fact Mama had the face of a steel kettle. Boiling inside. But without a whistle. Without a mouth either.

Years later, Mama would start or end some short no-end conversations with me this way, "Had I bent down and picked up my clothes and re-entered Kinta House, we would not have left for Tapioca House, and Mian would have . . ." Her eyes would turn mirror, without water.

And I never told Mama that walking down the main street that afternoon, I said repeatedly, inside, "*Ametofo* Buddha, this is Nin speaking, over, take me, Buddha, I am willing to pay for a happy family without the angry Godzilla, I am willing to die for a happy Mian, a happy Liang, a happy Mama, and a happy Pa, a happy and peaceful family in short, take me, you can take me, I don't mind death, can you hear me, Buddha, this is Nin speaking, over, today is my birthday, this is my wish today."

But I was selfish to the bone.

Not Mian. Me.

Buddha was drunk on December 31, 1981.

A short and straight rainbow marked the fresh-washed sky left behind by a brief and sudden monsoon that afternoon. No Buddha or angels could see. No Buddha or angels could see because the purple sky was rainbowed by a brilliant one. Very distracting. Very dangerous. No Buddha or angels could save Mian. Even the Biggest Angel was blinded by the brilliance of the rainbow. Even the almighty Allah of our Malay neighbors could not cancel December 31, 1981.

December 31, 1981. I started saving drowning ants from our rapid kitchen sink.

I still do.

"Now you know where the idea for my FireWife photo essay comes from. I want to do it in memory of my sister who drowned," I say. Softly.

Mahar, my husband, a caring but laconic man, shocked, puts his hand on my shoulder. I had wanted to but, for one reason or other, hadn't told him about the death of my sister throughout our seven-year marriage. The truth is I am guilty, I made Mian big and cock-eyed when she was only five, and she died.

As usual Mahar says nothing. But I feel his love through his grip on my shoulder. A steel net, always there, taking care, waiting to catch. But I am always kite-like, up down left right.

What I didn't tell Mahar is—I have a photograph of Mian when she died. Mama gave me the photo shortly after the funeral, she said she didn't want me to forget. How could I? No angels, not even Buddha or God or Allah, could breathe in tapioca mud. Mian was only five. But she must have tried. In the photo, her mouth and nostrils were stuffed stiff with white mud. No one knows, in my young years of sorrow, solace, and making sense, I studied the photograph every night. And every night, I plunged into the tapioca mud well voluntarily, quietly, maturely, after I closed the moist lids of my eyes. The plunge was always muddily white, dreamy, heavy, wet, pure, guilty. The white tapioca mud would enter my nostrils and throat. Once inside, the white mud would stay and grow fat. Then I would die like Mian did. And I would see Mian. And we would play like we used to. *Lost in Space*, of course. And every night Mian would laugh from eyebrow to eyebrow. She was so pretty, so fine. In the morning when I woke, I would wait for the next evening plunge to come. For years after Mian died, I studied the photo, I waited day and plunged night, waited and plunged, waited and plunged.

Now. Twenty-four years later. Sitting here in the bed-room in my home in San Diego, unbeknownst to my husband, Mahar, I can still feel the power of the photo from the next room, inside a desk drawer, inside a blank book smelling of sandalwood. The thought of Mian trapped in the photo in perpetual death erects my hair like trees standing stiff on skin. A zealous girlhood belief kicks in—Mian's soul must have gone with the photographer and become free. But little is known of the photographer now, once the supervisor at the tapioca factory. Some said he later left to work on a freight ship and died in an accident, some said he lost his legs, some said he left for Australia and contracted AIDS. But all knew he loved to travel and photograph, he brought only his cam-era when he left. I so want the photographer to be alive and well. Is he? I reach for Mahar's hands on my shoulder. His hands give me a comfort, immense and undivided, as usual.

Today is December 31. My thirty-first birthday.

My backpack is packed. In a few days, I'll leave Mahar and my home in San Diego for six months. Six months to travel from country to country and shoot a personal photo es-say I call FireWife. Six months' leave of absence from work. Enough is enough, I cannot and will not copy another E.D.I. Friday, I say to myself. For nine years now, I have worked as an architect for E.D.I. Friday, short for Every Day Is Friday. A relative newcomer to the casual dining restaurant business, E.D.I. Friday has surprised the industry by surpassing the market leader—T.G.I. Friday's—in almost all key markets three years in a row. Chief Architect for International Projects, my business card suggests, but I never refer to myself as one because the words *Chief Architect* scratch like bristled worms in my ears. I was in charge of duplicating E.D.I. Friday in Moscow, Shanghai, Seoul, Hanoi, Dubai, Osaka, Manila, Madrid, and Paris. Over the years, I duplicated and duplicated, just so I could travel, or more precisely, fly, especially in the empty night flights. Tied to a small seat by a belt on a plane, I would first see my sister in my mind's eye and I would feel guilty and die and heal and renew and see a new me outside, against the window, not an architect of any kind, not a sister, not a wife, not daughter, not woman, not friend, not worker, not stranger, not not stranger. Absolutely self-less. Yet absolutely self-centered. Absolutely guilt-free. History-free. Absolutely anonymous.

Now, I will embark on a *really* anonymous journey, free from work and the quotidian, to shoot moments in the lives of nameless girls and women. I will photograph the suffering, the unsure, the unfree, possibly also the seemingly sure and serene, to set the girls and women in my photographs free. I want to make real my girlhood belief that each of their spirits will leave behind a trapped body and start a journey as far and wide as the photographer's. But, no subject selection, no stages, no props in my journey. The magic can only work if I follow my instinct, go with the inner undertow, the flow.

The omnipresent Flow.

The fluid, shapeshifting Flow.

Tonight, the Flow is a sea with three folds. Near the surface is the same sharp tug at my heart every time I see a pool, a river, or a deep tub of suds, into which a girl, five years of age, can stumble and suffocate. This guilt keeps me grounded and cautious and sensible all the time all my life. This guilt spurs my desire to do FireWife. In memory of my sister who drowned. To free her somehow.

Yet I also want to do it to flee the grip of her death. Beneath the guilt is the acute urge to forget. Forget the image of Mian's body on a cot, still like a dead clock. But how does one leap off the solid cliff of memories and fly immensely? How does one become free as a fearless tiger with wings? FireWife will lead me to the key.

So will the third fold of Flow. For in this deepest layer lies my desire to escape everything that is routine in my life. A quest to fly carefreely, absolutely free from all guilts, all pieties, families, jobs, moral mores, and the daily needs to assemble who I am as expected and respected. A Fire Quest. Driven by a truer me long buried. But Fire Quest is curbed by Water Me gravitating toward groundedness, homestead, the conventional, the responsible, the good, the safe, the past.

I am married to Mahar, water, a doctor, dependable and kind and warm and gentle, skin subtly sweet like cumin and apple. I love him. And the world of fantasies, movies, books is where I have always gone to fly waywardly, as far and wide as the fire in me can imagine. But fantasies alone do not *really* expel the Water Me.

I must escape the Water Me I have become in the long grip of my sister's death to be the Fire Me, the truer me.

December 31. The eve of my FireWife journey. My thirty-first birthday.

Mahar has cooked me a fabulous dinner, he kisses me on my shoulder, he whispers, "Happy birthday, Nin, I love you dearly." My heart aches with tenderness. I trace the shape of his mouth with my thumb, yet I so long to begin my FireWife journey now. I finish the introspective champagne breathing like a contemplative fish in a tank. Across the TV blue screen, the new year is afire as the illuminated apple hesitantly chases away the old year. For a moment, I see the tail of the old year in between its legs, time too shivers at its own death, I could not have guessed. Mahar kisses me at the side of my neck near the ear. He kisses as if I would turn into a champagne bubble if he kissed me one ounce harder, and he whispers, "Happy New Year, Nin."

The first minute of the new year.

For a few strange moments, right after Mahar enters fully, I turn to look toward the big glass window, I see a smaller me sitting on a man's body, legs spread, waist straight, dizzy empty hungry.

Then I see a girl, in a flaming orange sari, with the glinting eyes of a tiger, a wee ball of fire between her brows, her face familiar and fine, entering me from behind, whispering Lakshmi . . . Lakshmi . . .

Who is she?

Fire Wife?

But a raging passion is surging at the bottom of my spine.

I close my eyes.

Suddenly I feel my old skin dying, shedding.

Every old inch of me.

Inch by inch I die.

And a new and ardent longing, huge as a sexing wave, ancient as fire needing air, needy as skin craving touch, begins to sex every inch of my new skin.

Sexing. Sexing.

New Me is coming.

But I remain a Can Be. At the moment of ecstasy.

in between
lives

———
———

In Genesis, Egg, Stable, Mother, Water were made
to stop Vessel from flying . . .
Innocent and Mirror were made to help Vessel
fly high and wide . . .
Man was made to burden Vessel with the weight
of posterity . . .
Ardor was the name of all objects of desire in
the bowl of Utopia . . .
THE MYTH

ZIMI: *Egg*

In Taipei

I am eighteen. My given name is Yun. I recently changed it to Zimi. Zimi is Purple Rice in Chinese. I picked Zimi because it is phonetically close to Jimi. I am a vocalist/song writer/guitarist in a rock band. My friends used to call me Jimi to mock me, but now they call me Jimi because they think I have the potential to become the Jimi Hendrix of Taiwan in the twenty-first century. Honestly I would rather be the next Melissa Etheridge. But it's hard to find a cool Chinese name that sounds like Melissa, so I am Zimi who wants to play like Hendrix and sing like Etheridge. My best quality is my honesty. I don't go for fad. I have my own stand on things. I am not humble. I am not proud. I am not above others. I am not below others. I don't drink. I don't smoke. I don't cut myself to feel. I don't do head-shaking pills. I don't sleep around. I own my own pace. I am a virgin and a celibate. But I do masturbate. My rule to life is simple: be true, be kind, but be true before be kind.

Kindness has many kinds. Pure kindness is hard to find. When you can't be pure in your kindness, it's better to know and be honest about the impurity in your kindness. I am not kind. My mother was. But she didn't know she was the kind of kind mother who needed you to stay dependent on her self-sacrificing kindness all your life. I was sad but relieved when she died, for in hindsight, I realize I had a plastic bag over my head when she was alive. But I never fault my mother for being a human, or for loving me too much. Loving mothers have a special spot in my heart. The way I see it: you come from one of their eggs inside, they give you life, they will die for you if they have to, it's only natural if you have a guilt or debt complex toward your mothers, you hope they don't do it this way but your mothers do have the right to suffocate you with love if they like.

I blossomed after my mother died. My rock band is doing more than fine. I don't play music for money. To foot the rent of my small den in the outskirts, by day I lease my forehead as advertising space in downtown Taipei. My forehead-as-ad-space business is good. Especially good after a reporter from Taiwan TV reported on me on the evening news. It's been especially good for three months now. Frankly I am surprised. Today I have "Tampax Tampons 2 for 1" on my forehead. Some smile when they see me. Some frown. The first-timers are often curious whether the words on my forehead are permanently tattooed. That is because I inscribe them in the tattoo style. See this frowning man who looks like President Ah Bian. He is the preacher from a church nearby. He gave me a lecture last week about body and temple and the holy spirit. As I listened to him preach, an enlightenment came upon me. Much like the moment Newton had when the apple hit his head, I suddenly understood why the Christians and the Muslims are at war more than the Buddhists. Buddhists have less compulsion to convert to save to civilize. Buddhists are less evangelical by nature, that's why. But no point in sharing your enlightenment with an agitated man who thinks you are damned and going to hell. So I asked the preacher if he wanted a haircut at Unisex 2006, a new salon two blocks away, 'cause last week I had Unisex 2006 on my forehead for a whole week.

Really, I have no qualm renting out my forehead, giving my eggs, feeding my dead body to fishes or birds, returning it to humus, donating my heart my liver my kidneys my corneas when I die. The way I see it: the body is more like a leaf or an egg. I love the idea of death in a leaf. When a leaf dies, it is airborne, it falls, it returns to earth, to its origin, its root. And I love the idea of life in an egg. An egg stores and gives life. An egg can hatch into a cute baby chick. Topped with ginger and scallion jimmies, an egg can turn into a bowl of nutritious egg flower soup. Egg flower soup is my life line. I believe a bowl of egg flower soup a day keeps the doctor away. And my mother was the one who told me about the eggs inside. She said when a girl has her first monthly blood and sheds the first egg in her life, she is left with 399,999 eggs inside. And what's left is enough to cover more than 30,000 years of monthly blood, that is more than 300 life times.

That's why (and it's not because I am kind) I am adamant about giving my eggs for free to an infertile friend of mine who can't afford to pay NT$200,000 per case of donor eggs. However many IVF cycles you need, I told her, I'll be there. I have 300 life times of egg supply. But last week, on the same day the preacher preached to me about body and temple, my friend's doctor refused to take me as an egg donor on the grounds that I am unmarried, eighteen, and a virgin. No, no, the doctor said, I can't take you, you are still a virgin, and you don't have 300 life times of egg supply, you have at best 30 years. And the doctor went on to give me a lecture on hymen, youth, regret, and the right time to do the right thing in life. He talked at length about how regretful women spent money to surgically restore their broken precious pieces of skin and how women who can't afford surgery use self-help hymen repair kits, the efficacy of which is dubious, he said. Little did he know, my resolve grew exponentially as he spewed out his views on what I will or will not regret in life.

I have a plan. I plan to break my virginal skin tonight. With a chopstick or my finger. And once I am no longer a virgin, the doctor will have to retrieve my eggs for my friend, though he will surely ask: WHY? WHY DID YOU DO IT? WHY? And I'll explain body is merely a part of Nature to be used and shared with care and respect, and frankly I don't see the point of worshiping a piece of membrane we call hymen that has no biological function, and I believe I do have 300 life times of egg supply.

chapter 4

NIN

Taipei → Bangkok

*D*o you know if you stare at a plane window long enough you can see the past?

Best is to try it with a window in a night plane. You must have a glass of port beforehand. One glass is more than ample. I have done this for years now. I can't can't do it. It's my ritual. Kick off my shoes. Wear the airline slippers. Order a glass of V8. Drink V8. Order a glass of port. Drink a glass of port. Be a-glass-of-port tipsy. Eat a packet of airline peanuts. Stare into the window. Look.

Pa is floating in the sea below outside the window. He is also eating some peanuts. He is eating his favorite Wang Li Wang peanuts, the kind you must crack the shell before you can get to the nuts. He eats his peanuts with much effort. He is floating and shelling peanuts at the same time. He doesn't know that I am watching him from the window of a plane. He doesn't know that I am flying to Bangkok now.

Pa is waving at my plane. I don't think he sees me.

Pa once told me that the much-thumbed 1963 edition of the *Oxford Advanced Learner's Dictionary of Current English* was next to his pillow for years and that's how he self-taught and became proficient in the language of English. Pa was also fluent in Chinese, Bahasa Malaysia, and Thai. Really, Nin, he said, if you are as diligent as Pa, you can become anything you want to be, you can even become the first Chinese and female Prime Minister of Malaysia. So, if you think this big one is too formidable, he encouraged, start with a smaller dictionary.

Pa is shelling and eating and trying to float at the same time. He doesn't know that I am watching him from the plane. He doesn't know that I did begin one winter morning in college in the U.S., in memory of him, to pound *a, aah, aardvark, aardwolf, Aaron, Aaronic* from a Merriam-Webster's dictionary into my brain. Six words a day. Every day. I came close to giving up at *carpophore* but managed to reach *castigate.*

And only *castigate.*

A broken piece of airline nut tickles my throat.

I cough.

Look.

Pa is gone. Only his rubber sandals are floating on the face of the sea now. They go round and round. Rounding. Rounding to the closest zero as though zero is something easier to grasp. Or something more profound. The sea is calm.

Peanut is a symbol of longevity. Malaysian Chinese eat

peanuts to celebrate new years and birthdays. But Pa didn't live to be forty-three.

I believe Pa took his own life so that he could be with Mian. Pa's hair turned completely vermicelli silvery overnight the day Mian died. Mian was his peanut, pinkpink, baby girl, sunshine, bububee, dragonhead, and sweet-eyes. He called me Nin and only Nin all the time.

But many believed Pa accidentally drowned. He had no reason to kill himself, they said. He was too responsible a man. Plus, his daughter Mian had died so long ago, he must have healed, they said it as though it was a matter of biological fact. They said it because they themselves had forgotten, healed, and moved on.

In high school, I was remembered as the girl whose father drowned while fishing with friends on the Strait of Malacca. But I was a girl whose younger sister drowned and whose father chose to drown himself.

The policeman, too, ruled that Pa's death was accidental, not self-chosen. He said it as though accidental deaths were better than self-chosen deaths. In the name of rectitude, the policeman repeated his view.

But I know. Pa chose to die. He called me Nin and only Nin all the time.

Pa's death, the second Hour of Lead in my life, was light as air in a bubble.

It was insignificant.

It was wrongfully insignificant.

I couldn't feel. So I didn't cry.

But I picked up where Pa left off.

I began liking peanuts very much.

I became a peanut connoisseur, like him. I know my peanuts very well.

I also began skipping peanuts that are four nuts in one shell.

Four is death, Pa would say.

Pa would also say: you are my eldest child, Nin, even though you are a girl, I treat you like a boy, an eldest son must take his father's place when his father's gone. And I would ask: where you going? And he would say: no place, just in case. And every time I would assure him and shout out No Problem, Pa! with a chestful of confidence, like a responsible man in the making, like a girl who has long curbed her Small Me into oblivion.

Really, now, when I look into the window of a night plane long enough, I see a familiar pattern in my past—a pattern of wanting to be small and carefree but having to be and being big and careful all the time. My history is one of wanting to be Small Me/Fire Me but having to be and being Big Me/Water Me.

Pa is grinning in the sea. He is probably grinning at a school of fish around him.

I also picked up Pa's hobby of fishing. Off the bank, not deep-sea fishing like Pa had done with his friends on the Strait of Malacca. Now, I still fish when I have a breather and need a piece of peace. Fishing hones my sense of waiting, almost always for nothing. Waiting for nothing makes me make peace with predictable routines, like the seasons at a CVS or a Walgreens—Cupid, Bunny Rabbit, Pumpkin, Santa Claus, Cupid, Bunny Rabbit, Pumpkin.

I also began shooting photographs with Pa's camera. Yashica. And I would hear him say, listen to your eyes, Nin, listen to your eyes. Pa would've been pleased with the FireWife project I have in mind. I listen to my eyes. Like yesterday in downtown Taipei, I heard the adamance wrought up in the face and body of a young woman who had "Tampax Tampons 2 for 1" tattooed on her forehead. I took a photograph of her, her tenacious face happy and smooth like an egg. I felt connected to her somehow, I can't explain it, I could feel a tension somewhere on her face, in her space, wrought up in her body, her history, waiting to release, and I could relate. The girl, her name is Zimi, she insisted on telling me her story. She said she likes the idea of death in a leaf. She said when a leaf dies, it falls, it returns to its origin, a leaf on the ground will turn into nutrients to birth new things. I feel like a leaf now, airborne, in limbo, in between, at once ending and starting, dying and birthing.

Leaf or not, I listened to my eyes like Pa had taught me: if my eyes feel and hear a tension, a bond, I turn to look and take a picture if I can.

Look. Outside the plane window now.

Pa is bobbing again in the sea.

He sees me. He is smiling. He seldom smiled.

He gives me a thumbs-up. A thumbs-up is the trademark of Wang Li Wang peanuts in shell. Is he giving me a thumbs-up because I listen to my eyes like he had taught me? Or because he sees a tear creeping from my eye into my mouth?

It's a tear of knowledge. Not of sadness.

It's a tear of knowing death.

They say life is keen in the face of death.

But the knowledge of death grounds me instead. I can't and don't fly freely, waywardly, let alone keenly.

I am merely . . .

I am merely finishing dying.

Finish dying is a phrase I became fixated upon in one of Samuel Beckett's stories.

Samuel Beckett had sword eyes. Despite my awe for Beckett, I have never fancied men with sword eyes. Sword eyes make you see the insignificance in existence and what you are made to see will suck dry your sense of self, goal, vanity, bearing, pride.

On the airline TV screen on the back of the seat in front of me now, Russell Crowe appears. Russell Crowe has the eyes of displaced nature, wayward wind, the eyes of dangerous ardor. Not sword. He has a wing-tipped upper lip.

The man next to me in 3B puts on his airline TV earphones. 3B is extremely perfumed. Diorissimo. Diorissimo is a seriously feminine perfume. Does cross-perfuming suggest a penchant for cross-dressing? 3B has a much dog-eared *The Story of O* on his lap. *The Story of O! The Story of O* was the bible of my college best friend, Lara Flyer.

Lara was a transfer sophomore from Bates; she said she transferred to Wellesley because she was tired of Maine. Just before our junior year, after having read *The Story of O* fifty times or so, Lara dated a married man from Natick for a whole summer. Based on her experience with the married man, Lara declared that she liked giving more than receiving spanking. She also said that the s-hole (she gestured a tight o with all her fingers in one hand) is at least five hundred times more profound than the v-hole (she gestured a narrow v with two fingers), to which, she added, really, it is a business of not merely the whole asshole but the whole ass and hole. Then she said, Nin, if you are ever curious about how to *fly* immensely and where your G-spot is, ask me. Upon hearing such wonder, I accidentally dropped the can of V8 in my hand onto my summer dress. Lara raised her V8 and declared: To the emancipation of Nin's pious cherry and pit, a defloration in nutritious splendor, my friend, this is a good omen indeed. Cheers to Genesis, she said. Then she took off her clothes and ran into the lake by which we were sitting. Lara had the figure of Kate Winslet and the face of Élodie Bouchez. She had papaya breasts. She, the wild one, asked me to skinny-dip with her in the water, but I, the proper one, remained seated with my dress doused in tomato red.

Cheers to the breaking of Nin's chrysalis! Lara cried from the lake.

I wanted to be winged. But how?

And here I am, years later, the past seeps changelessly into the present: I want to be winged. But how?

Outside the plane window now a thin V8-red sliver cuts across the smoky silk sky. Above the sliver, I see Lara and me meeting for the first time in Professor Stone's popular class— Literature of the Absurd. Class participation accounted for fifty percent of the grade, and I spoke once and only once in class, but I spoke at length, at length about the idea of "finish dying" in Samuel Beckett's *Molloy*. After class, Lara came up to me and called me Hey FD. Short for Finish Dying, she said. Impromptu, I called Lara Flyer Hey FL. Short for Finish Living, I said. And we became friends. Among the many differences we discovered we had, it turned out that we shared a common love for Suzanne Vega and V8. And our ears shared the same odd shape.

Superimposed upon the window face of Lara now is 3B trying to insert his *Story of O* into the full mouth of his seat pocket. He riffles, unsuccessfully.

I turn from the plane window.

Russell Crowe appears again on my tiny TV screen.

Is doing Russell Crowe a way to become winged? I feel my lips turn doused red.

Look.

Outside the plane window, above the glass red sliver, I see a Russell Crowe bending down. Or is he Tony Leung? Or Denzel?

I squint my tipsy eyes.

Whoever he is, he is bending down very slowly.

He is bending down to kiss my mouth.

I guess my window eyes can see not only the past but also what I mustn't but want to in real life.

chapter 5

Ut: *Innocent*

In Bangkok

Ut, you idiot you. Smile, damn it! Can't you see the white men walking by?"

I am Ut. Today is my birthday. I don't feel like smiling today.

I think Mamasan has the world's most diligent carping tongue. I hate her. She was also the one who told us that we can't get AIDS because we are female, and only homosexuals and white people get AIDS. But thousands of red pox chewed away Pong's face, bit by bit. Red pox also drank her blood, in sips. I am glad Pong is with Buddha now. I hate Mamasan. She insists that Pong died because she peed on some tree gods somewhere. And she still insists on us wearing no condoms if the men don't want to. We ask, "What about us?" She says, "No business, no us." Shrugs her shoulders and walks away. I hate Mamasan. But then, all Mamasans are alike. At least this Mamasan gives us an herb drink every other day to protect us from AIDS. "Just in case," she says. She drinks it too. I hope this herb drink is Buddha-sent and works. Everyone drinks it now. Still, I hate Mamasan very much.

"Sawadeekah. I am Ut. Number 32." I have been saying this for two years now. Two long years. Enough to grow a callus in my private part.

Today feels like a day of nine suns. Beads of sweat smile at me from the tip of my nose. Today is Tuesday. It has been a slow day. I like it this way. I can dream and talk. There are so many beautiful things outside under the sun. Among them I pick a different listener every day. I am very picky about whom I pick. She or he has to feel right to me. I talked to a passing gray-bottom cloud once. She was great. And the old, peeling fire hydrant sitting outside our display window reminds me of my father. I call him Mr. Fire Eater. He has a pair of loyal ears. I can talk to him anytime I want to. He is always here.

But today I am talking to you. Yes you, the fly with green-red eyes. You are one of us. You are caught in the display window, too. Can I call you Noi? How are you today, Noi? You are my lucky listener of the day. You are especially lucky, because today is my birthday.

You know, Noi, I love to daydream about my flower cart. I have been saving twenty baht a week for two years now. This saving is for me and me only. I want my flower cart to be as big as a cow cart.

Noi, do you know why I am mute outside? I am especially mute toward Mamasan. I am afraid if I open my mouth to talk to her I might accidentally spit in her face. That is not wise. I will wait until the day I buy my flower cart. That will be the day I cough vomit onto her face. Take a good look at her face. That is the face of a donkey next life. I assure you of that.

Since Pong died, I have no more sister-friends. We used to go to temple three times a week. We shared everything, like real blood-sisters. We used to talk and talk and talk. Sometimes with our eyes. Sometimes with our mouths. To tell you the truth, Noi, I felt that we talked better with our eyes, like now. Sitting in this box window, we didn't like to talk with our mouths.

I am Ut. I am also number 32. Today is my birthday. I turn fourteen today. How old are you, Noi? You know, I still sleep in a fetus way. Nobody believes that I remember my mama's womb, but I do. She was warm like a bowl of jasmine rice. Do you believe me? I hope you do. I always wish that I can tell the customers: "Please let me lie on my right side, please." I curl on my right side. I can't sleep any other way. I love my straw mat at home. It is homey and close to earth. When I am here lying on a bed, I try to think of my straw mat at home and my mama's face and the warm jasmine pudding she made.

You know, Noi, my mama had pure Chinese blood in her, even though she looked like pure Thai. She was our village's best massager. She had a pair of potato-thumbs that could squeeze the sickest wind out of the deepest nook inside the oldest man. But when Mama fell ill, there were no other equally gifted thumbs to flatten the sick knots inside her. Her stomach grew to the size of a table. A dark stone table. It was as if my mama were cursed with nine babies and then some. But she died with a smile. She said she was paying all of the debts from her last life, and her children's debts as well.

I am Ut. Ut is my first name. I don't have a family name, I say. People will spit on my family name if I tell it. I don't want that to happen. But you look like you really want to know. Well, my last name is Bangkok. Yes, Bangkok. I gave it to myself on my twelfth birthday. I am Bangkok Ut. Number 32.

Westerners have a funny way of saying things. They call Bangkok the Angel City. They say we are angels. I don't see how. Don't all angels have long blond hair, big blue eyes, and sand white skin? Angels hold sticks with yellow stars on them. I saw an angel once when I was small, in my sister's schoolbook. The angel pointed her stick to the earth and the earth started to spit out loaves and loaves of bread for a poor girl to bring home. I am Thai. I don't look like an angel. I don't eat bread. I don't hold a stick with a yellow star on it. This American guy, right? He paid me to be his Thai wife for two weeks. He called me "honey sugar angel bun." White men must like angels very, very much.

Today is my birthday, Noi. I am fourteen today. I went to the temple to talk to Buddha early this morning. I brought him eight clusters of yellow jasmine. Noi, have you flown in a temple before? It is a happy place. Do go. Buddha has a kind face and very long earlobes. My earlobes are short and slim; they explain why I am here. Did you know that fat earlobes can bring you good luck, and can fan bad luck off your path? Do you have a pair of earlobes, too? I mean, do flies have ears? How many ears? If so, I hope your earlobes are as big as your toes. Do you have toes? Anyway, do go pay Buddha a visit sometime. I asked Buddha to give good grades to my younger sisters and brothers. Especially Nit. My youngest sister. She is smart but she likes to cheat.

You know, Noi, I also asked Buddha if he gave my mama a good next life. Last night, I dreamed that Mama had a third eye. It sat between her brows. A tear rushed down from her third eye and curved around her nose into her mouth. The fortune-teller outside the temple explained to me that my mama is a people-buddha now. Her kind deeds in her massager life earned her a wise eye. I am glad. But the fortune-teller didn't say why my mama's wise eye cried. I hope Buddha gave my mama a good next life.

And I also asked Buddha to cure my papa's spine. A crooked wind lives in his back. His back trembles like an aged hammock, sometimes weakly, sometimes madly. But Papa insists on working, bicycling around sharpening scissors and knives of folks in nearby towns. I just spent four hundred baht on more anise bandages, but even these best bandages with anise mud have failed to pluck the vile wind off his spine. I am witless on this one, Noi. I am worried about my papa. I hope Buddha will help me soon.

You know, Noi, sometimes I actually feel very lucky. Lucky because I am not one of the performer girls next door. I don't think I can live very long if I have to do "fire stick in pussy" show or "pussy smoke cigarette" show or "pussy with Ping-Pong ball" show or "pussy chop banana" show or "pussy writing with a fountain pen" show or "pussy opening bottle of Coca-Cola" show. They even have a "pussy shooting darts" show. I don't know why men cheer in ecstasy when seeing women in danger.

Mamasan once said that rooster fighting, kickboxing, "pussy razor thrilling" show are all the same. She said it is human nature to pay a lot of money to taste danger and to see bloodshed. Not me. I know you agree with me, too, Noi. I think performer girl has it much, much worse than boxers or roosters. Roosters and boxers are heroes. People respect them very much. Especially the roosters.

Come to think of it, a flower cart is not good enough. I must tell Buddha that I want to be a man next life. Then I can open my own factory. I can hire boys and girls, train them and pay them well. I will become rich and powerful and burn down all the brothels and build hundreds of schools. My schools will give free books, free shoes, free lunches. Of course, I must not forget to spit on Mamasan's face if she remains her old self. I must ask Buddha this on Thursday.

Today is my birthday. I am fourteen today.

Look at him, Noi. Yeah, the white man wearing a green-yellow batik shirt. I have a feeling he is going to stop and come in. Yes, he stops. He turns. His eyeballs roll from left to right. His breath grows a tiny ball of fog on the outside of the window, between his eyes and us. He takes a step to the left. See his face, Noi? He has the who-the-hell-are-Jesus-Buddha-Mohammed-I-am-in-heaven-oh-oh-my-mama look. I have a feeling he may take a while to decide among the four of us girls in this window.

I think he is going to pick me. His eyes are drooling. His lips are saying, Number 32.

I'll tell you a secret, Noi: Fly forward two yards, then go another three yards to your right, and you will see the door. You will be free. Outside. Outside the display window. You will be right in the middle of Bangkok, under a sky of nine suns. There are many beautiful things under the sun. Outside the window, I mean. Now fly away as fast as you can. Bye, Noi. Bye, fly. I hope I won't see you again in here. Sorry I forgot to listen to what you may have wanted to say about your life. I hope you don't mind. Today is my birthday. I am fourteen today.

"Sawadeekah. I am Ut. Number 32."

chapter 6

NIN

Bangkok → Tokyo

*D*ream. When I dream during a flight, I often levitate or fly.

"Is Buddha a woman?" I ask, balancing on an airline-pillow-size cloud.

"Yes and no," Mama says, levitating on a small cloud herself. "Buddha is androgynous."

"You mean like the top a woman, the bottom a man?" I ask. I see a pink kite fluttering nearby.

"Not exactly," Mama replies, "more like you and me, more like our yin-yang face. It's not a top-bottom difference but a left-right balance. Take your face for instance, the left side of your face is more female than your right and your right more male. It is the same with Buddha. No matter, Buddha is by your side, Nin, you were born unafraid."

"But I am always careful and afraid," I say.

"No, you were born unafraid! You were born with the Buddha earlobes," Mama insists, caressing my earlobes.

An acute sense of confidence and bliss showers upon me.

But bliss is bliss because it is brief.

A long plateau of bliss is no bliss.

Lara, my college best friend, once proclaimed that she would choose a short moment of sharp bliss over a long plateau of blunt bliss anytime. "But you, Nin," she said, "I bet you would choose otherwise. You know why? Because you are in the habit of eating for sustenance and I for pleasure." She paused, her eyes looking deep into mine, then she said, "But there is something unrestrained and hungry in your eyes, Nin. Deep inside your pupils, that something looks like a girl on fire." She frowned, squinted, blinked, and so did I. Lara continued her diagnosis. "You know what I think, Nin? When you are done eating for sustenance, you may turn out to be the biggest eater of pleasure." Lara looked like a scientist cautiously making sense of her lab mouse.

I looked away from her eyes and declared, "My choice is simple. It would depend on how blunt blunt bliss is and how sharp sharp bliss is. It would also depend on what happens after a moment of sharp bliss ends. Does sharp bliss end with sharp grief? Or where sharp bliss ends blunt bliss begins? If it is the latter, Lara, believe me, I am all for eating for pleasure."

Zooooooooooooop! A wayward cloud, rose red in hue, swallows the pink kite! Pink kite is gone! Kaput. I scream. And scream and scream until my eardrums become so scared they evaporate, my earlobes so worried they wilt. And wilt and wilt and I hold tight my wilting ears and scream, "Please save my good earlobes, somebody save my good earlobes please!"

Mama bends down from her piece of cloud. Again, she assures me that I was born good-eared, strong, brave. Then she gives me my favorite plum candy wrapped in rice paper. I put it in my mouth. It is sweet and sour. The rice paper begins to melt in my saliva. "Ma, have you found peace?" I ask, my tongue sweet and sour.

"Peace is found only when and where there is war. There is no war where I am now, so there is no need for peace." She changes the subject. "I saw your pa the other day."

I look around and Pa is nowhere to be found.

"Pa is dead," I say, levitating on my small cloud.

"I know that," Mama says in an even tone. "But you know what he did? He had the sheer gall to enter my dream and tell me that he doesn't want to see me ever again in his next life or next next life or next next next life! Not again, he said."

Pa is his same old must-have-the-last-word self—quick to put down, dismiss, hurt with his words just so that he can savor the bliss of having a brief upper hand in a conflict. And Mama hasn't found peace. The thought gives my heart a violent jig almost enough to tumble me off my small pearly cloud. The jig was the same shuddering, nauseating feeling I had every time Pa and Mama fought when I was growing up, that was when Pa was still with us. Pa was an irascible man. His fury, directed only at his wife and the Malaysian government's mistreatment of Malaysian Chinese, began when Mian died. Mama was a soft-spoken and strong woman. Her self-defensive fury, passive and quiet, but as intense, directed only at her husband and herself, also began on the day Mian died.

In short, on the day I made Mian big and cock-eyed, and she died, the God of Furious Quarrel entered our house and stayed furious for years to come.

I took statistics of Mama's and Pa's bitter bickering once, for a whole month. They fought, big and small, five days a week, on average.

So, I ask Mama, "So, you guys fought in the dream?" Dizzy in anticipation, I park my jigging cloud by wedging it against hinges of the sky.

"No, your pa and I are beyond that. But I did tell him, if I ever bump into him in my next lives, likewise, I will run like the sky is falling upon my head, he can be sure of that!"

Couples are supposed to quarrel at the head and make up at the foot of their beds. That's what the Malaysian Chinese believe. The way I see it, though: Pa and Mama seldom reached the foot of their bed. As a matter of fact, the year I entered high school, they began to sleep on beds separated by a nightstand, like Lucy and Ricky in *I Love Lucy* on TV.

"That's the problem," I whisper, "you guys are always making statements, making exclamations."

"What? Nin, I can't hear what you said. There is mist between us now," Mama says.

I repeat myself, louder. "I said you and Pa are always making exclamations. How do you expect to connect exclamation to exclamation? Exclamatory statements are by nature stand-alone. They destroy conversation. They enhance no connection." Imagine a man trying to pick up a woman with only exclamatory remarks.

Mama's face is veiled by the thickening mist when she says, "As usual, Nin, you take your father's side."

"No, Ma"—I am eager to explain everything—"that's not true, I love you more than I love Pa. Pa is dead—why are you still saying this?" I feel light-headed. There is the smell of cuttlefish jerky in the air.

"Go ahead and love your pa more," Mama replies. "I have found inner peace at the temple. Nothing can stir me anymore."

There must have been inner war for Mama to have found inner peace.

Another gust of cuttlefish jerky wafts by. My head begins to spin. And before I can further explain myself, my small cloud begins to fall.

I twitch to stop my falling. But in vain.

Dream. That's right, I fall and twitch often in my airplane dreams.

. . .

The man sitting next to me in 5B is at most nineteen. Possibly Japanese. Seeming an up-and-coming pop star, he looks like he belongs not in Business Class but in his own private jet. His left side profile is pleasing to the eyes. Very Keanu Reeves. A package of half-consumed cuttlefish jerky pinned stiffly in his seat pocket. 5B is engrossed in a manga in his hands. But look, I suspect 5B has led an unshielded life thus far. Look at his ear, yes, his left ear, the only ear I can see, there is no earlobe here. No earlobes to help dispel danger from his path.

Robert Downey Jr. is almost earlobe-less. So was Carolyn Bessette.

The girl prostitute whom I photographed in Bangkok, number 32, standing inside a boxed-in window, she has earlobes as tiny as mung beans. I hope a copy of her spirit managed to leave with me, fleeing her boxed-in misery.

Really, the wee-earlobe list goes on to include thousands whose lives were un-written, un-photographed, un-filmed, whose sufferings and deaths were un-remembered, un-thought-of, un-heard, unsung, unnamed.

My small sister, Mian, please remember her, she died when she was only five, and her earlobes were the size of the tip of a chopstick. And you could hardly call my father's earlobes august.

And because Mama's earlobes are narrow as rice, so, two years after Pa's death, a few months before I was leaving for college in the U.S. on full financial aid, Mama decided to shed all in life that is pleasurable, comfortable, material. I mean all. No TV. No movies. No novels of any type. Mama was a voracious reader of novels. No picnic by the beach. No meat. No comfortable bed. No onion, no leek, no garlic. No lipsticks. No colorful skirts. No sex. No Teresa Teng's love songs. No killing of mosquitoes even if they are standing stiff on your skin. Mama hugged me to her chest, and I could smell her armpits, faintly sweet like sandalwood. Mama said, "I am a four-legged table, each of you a table leg—Mian, Liang, your pa, and you. I don't know how to live a balanced life on two legs. Do you understand, Nin? There are wars in my head. I need a peaceful place to rest my mind. Good-Grandma will take care of Liang when I'm gone. You are my eldest child, I know you will be fine. You were born strong and unafraid."

"But I am always afraid and careful," I said, unburying my head from her chest.

"No, Nin, you were born unafraid, careless and unafraid," Mama said. "You were born to sap. Take. Not give. You caused the accident, remember?" A chilling guilt ran down my spine. I made Mian big and cock-eyed, and she died. I was the killer. Ground me, I whispered inside, punish me, I refuse to be freed. Mama hugged me tighter. "You must learn to give, Nin. Give love that doesn't hurt, love that is not careless, not selfish."

Then I heard Mama say, "Take good care of yourself when you are in America. Work hard. America is cold. At night, always cover your tummy with a blankie. Wear warmly.

And don't sit on men's beds. Don't sit on any man's bed. And don't watch too many movies or too much TV. Study!" She said it as though we were parting for life.

Two days after we talked, Mama cut her long hair to ear length and left to become a Buddhist nun at a temple in Taiping. It was February when Mama left, an unusually dry February day; the air felt as though it had been smothered and desiccated into powder. As she walked into the temple with her head tilted slightly to catch a glimpse of us at the corner of her eye, I saw her exposed earlobe narrow and pale as rice.

I have come to believe in portly earlobes. Two fat earlobes, plump as toes, can protect you from ruinous luck. They can also give you guiltless peace and plenty. They can make you guiltlessly free.

Believe me, double-fat earlobes double the auspiciousness.

Bill Gates, said to make two million dollars an hour, has pearl-onion earlobes.

So did Julia Child. So do Emeril, Ming Tsai, and Jacques Pépin.

Alan Greenspan has earlobes as big as Buddha's. Believe me, under his earful watch, the economy can never spiral into a second Great Depression.

And I married Mahar in part because he has a pair of earlobes as corpulent as thumbs and ears the size of palms.

As for mine. I had my fortune read once, only once, in

Boston Chinatown. Upon seeing my ears, the fortune-teller declared, "Your life is unpredictable because your ears are unpredictable. But one thing is sure, you should have died when you were a child. The smaller the ear cups the shorter the life. Yours are tiny. But you are lucky. You were shielded from death by your fat earlobes. You must treat your lucky earlobes well. Oil them. Don't puncture them with earrings, don't clip on them anything fancy or glittering. And your future will depend on how your ear cups and your earlobes interlock. If your fat earlobes have the upper hand, you will be in the upper room of luck. If your tiny ear cups have the upper hand, you will be in the lower room of luck. When people have big earlobes, they have big ear cups. Odd ears you have."

I was more than tongue-tied. Did Mian die . . . in my place? My earlobes, the culprits, felt heavy as mud. Instantly. My head was emptying. Rapidly. The block of guilt in my chest rose to wall size.

Outside the fortune-teller joint, I stood in the narrow alley for a while that winter afternoon. Quivering. Incessantly. The winter winds were tiny knives slashing my face my body. Then I puked. Then a two-legged cat, having struggled from the deep belly of the alley, lay by my side, lowered its head, and began chowing down my puke. I ran like a nerve-struck thoroughbred.

It was my first and last visit to a fortune-teller.

Lara, who had my shape of ears, didn't believe what I told her about our ears. Cow dung! she said.

But it's the earlobes, really.

Al Gore lost to George W. Bush by an earlobe. Trust me.

And President Clinton, how shall I explicate? Basically, had he had earlobes as big as quail eggs, he could have been swallowed by Monica Lewinsky and no one would have noticed.

In short, short ears short life, long ears long life, big earlobes big luck, small earlobes small luck, and big ears that are taller than the eyebrows bestow on their owners clout.

Mine are short life, big luck, little clout.

I don't care about clout. But shouldn't life be freer, keener when life is peppered with big luck and death is destined to be sooner than desired?

Keener how? Freer how?

Can one live freely and passionately and safely and responsibly, simultaneously?

Passionately safe. Safely passionate.

5B has just gotten a paper cut from the manga he is reading.

He sucks his paper-cut finger.

The plane slumps.

He sucks his finger again.

The plane slumps again.

And again. And again.

He stops sucking his finger.

The plane continues to slump in steps.

5B's manga flies out of his hand.

I look out the plane window.

Our plane is wingless! What happened to the wing?

Is our plane wingless or one-winged?

5B asks, "Would you like a piece of my cuttlefish jerky before we hit the ground?"

"What? You are offering me a piece of cuttlefish jerky now?"

Grinning, 5B says, "Life is short, especially right now, take a bite, you may be surprised."

I never liked cuttlefish jerky despite its popularity in Malaysia where I grew up. But in college, I was the one who bought Lara, a French Canadian, born and raised near Cummins Pond, New Hampshire, her first packet of cuttlefish jerky from the Yangzi Grocery Store in Boston Chinatown after she told me she loved everything and anything calamari. And Lara became severely hooked on cuttlefish jerky. The first time she went out with the married man from Natick, she told me she pulled down his pants and boxer shorts and his pecker exuded the pungent smell of cuttlefish jerky. She had a good feast, she said in glee. Live free or die, you must try it sometime, she said.

I pull a shred of 5B's cuttlefish jerky from the packet and put it in my mouth.

The smell of a sexual sea. I feel queasy.

I am spiraling in a quickening gyre now.

5B has freed himself from his seat belt.

5B is whirling faster than I am.

The whole plane is caught in a giant gyre now.

5B looks like Keanu Reeves in *The Matrix.* Twisting like a twister. Dodging drops of port, pillows, bags, cups, laptops, napkins, peanuts, oxygen masks.

He is still holding the packet of cuttlefish jerky, like he's holding a gun.

A handsome happy smile on his face.

"What is so fucking happy?" I ask 5B, in despair.

But look, 5B has no right ear. One-eared he is.

Holy Monkey! I am sitting next to a one-eared man.

Oh, Buddha, please help me arrive safely into Tokyo because one thing is sure—every ear is a cipher and of every ear there is a theme.

And of every one-eared man there is a theme of imbalance.

The imbalance of a one-winged plane.

"Wake up, earlobes!" I scream. I slap my lucky earlobes hard.

"Fight for the upper hand, damn it! I need the upper room of luck. Now!"

Falling, I rub earnestly my fluttering fat earlobes. "Come on! Come on!! Fly me to the upper room of luck. Come on!!!"

Dream. That's right, I always fall in the end of my airplane dreams.

. . .

I twitch. I open my eyes.

There is cuttlefish jerky in the air. *Really.*

My head is spinning.

I turn to get a glimpse of the man sitting next to me, 5B.

His left side profile is very Keanu Reeves.

5B is belted safely to his seat.

He is eating cuttlefish jerky and reading manga at the same time.

5B has just had a paper cut from the manga he is reading.

Déjà vu. Am I still in the dream?

Sincerely, how does one *really* know where one is in layers of realities?

How does one *really* know one's exact location in the big scheme of things?

chapter 7

TABLE: *Stable*

In Tokyo

One hundred years ago a man planted his dragon seed into my womb, but I didn't see his face and couldn't tell if his eyes were almond or button shaped, and days tiptoed by and every night I sat in my bed let down my hair and let loose the five-yard cloth-python around my belly, and every night I put into a jade box the emerald-dragonfly-barrette-with-golden-eyes, and every night I counted with my toes and fingers the number of cloths I weaved and embroidered all my life, and every night it neared twenty ten-fingers and twenty ten-toes, and a smile immediately flooded the valley between my lips until the dream leaped into my eyes, and every dawn my eyes full of eyes men's eyes women's eyes uncles' eyes aunts' eyes, so full of disgust they popped, and arrows of spit penetrated my smooth face and went out through the back of my head and pierced millions of shame-holes on the wooden wall, and shame-holes sucked cold wind into my grain-size room and froze my red blood behind my head into red crystals red flakes, and shame-holes drained away my family name, and my father's sighs my mother's tears were helpless ghosts with caring palms holding red crystals red flakes, and every dawn an old dream leaped into my eyes, and days tiptoed by until I poked a sharpened bamboo stick into the softness between my legs, and the bamboo tearing its way deeper and deeper until it pierced through the temple of the dragon seed and nailed the pumping heart and a joy cry vomited itself through my mouth and nostrils, and I wondered why can't the penis be as gentle as this bamboo stick, and I imagined my freedom a wild sword-orchid in pure right in pure confidence in pure solitude in pure ecstasy, and right away I made up my mind I would not settle for less than a woman warrior in my next life, and I thought a woman dragonfly would be the best.

One hundred years later three hundred and sixty-five days a year, I take off my turquoise-dragonflies-drinking-honey-on-the-horizon-of-a-lily-pond kimono, and right away all four men cheer and clap and drool and almost wet their pants, and their eyes chew on my nipples and their noses leave their faces onto my essence, and I lie down among them and I close my eyes, and I start praying to my dead mother who was a Chinese born in Japan, who sold her body to pay our country's war debts, and now I sell my body as a table to put sushi on to be eaten from, and I pray to Buddha but Buddha is too busy with the starving and the shoeless and the footless this week, and I hate the waiter who likes to call me Table and who places tiger-eye-sushi-rolls on my nipples, and I quarrel with him every time and every time he comes with every tooth sneering in his mouth, and every time he puts four tiger eyes on one nipple and four on the other, and I imagine a chi-spit that I have diligently practiced goes through the space between his brows and a blood-fountain shoots out and kills the four monstrous mouths and I cheer inside, but every time my small smile wilts as the chopsticks start to move, and I zip my lips with pride as chopsticks walk my naked pale breasts, and I dress like a bride in colorful sushi and a soy sauce river carrying wasabi sand slowly snakes into my navel into a small black-green sea in which red-yellow sashimi bathes before flying kamikazely through sharp tobacco teeth of four grotesque mouths, and men's cold saliva blended with hot sake drizzles onto my numb-no-more-goose-bumps belly, and stock prices' up-down and how Mr. Tanaka gave the boss the fanciest gift for Christmas try to sneak into my ears but fail, and I lie there every night imagining sipping a cup of rice tea in a Japan Airlines jet flying to New York City to study fashion design while my nose fighting a rotten tuna fish, and I remember a joke that says the three most pampered beings on earth are Japanese men and British dogs and American women, and I think why the joke a joke and for whom I will fight for the right to be in the next life, and I decide every night I will fight to be a woman dragonfly.

Nin

Tokyo → Singapore

*O*utside the plane infinite black is pregnant with tales untold.

Inside humans are housed like plants in a portable greenhouse in transit.

I don't need to know how to shape-shift. But the ability to place-shift is a nice know-how to know now. Now.

My yoga teacher back in San Diego, whose family name is Butman, would say: place-shifting depends on your ability to concentrate your mind. I would argue otherwise, for I have known how to mentally place-shift for a long time now; it does not require your ability to concentrate your mind; you need only to soften your body and let go of your eyes. Mentally place-shifting, in other words, is having a mental vacation—you are in Hawaii at your desk in downtown L.A. at 3 p.m. but you are *not really* in Hawaii. I call this thought mechanism SPLIT. Short for splitting to a mental vacation.

It's like your front brain is still data-entering a worksheet but your back brain is yippee I am snorkeling in Hawaii.

I don't remember when and how I learned to SPLIT so well—essentially anytime, anywhere, anyhow. As a teenage girl, at night in bed, I would often SPLIT to see a long-legged girl acrobat, gliding back and forth, suspended low to a full audience who would fight to kiss the candy the circus man put in between my legs, and I would lie in bed as though I were dead but dead happy, not dead sad. And then there were nights in bed when I would SPLIT to *Space: 1999* where I was sheltered by the indestructible Eagle One, and loved and protected by three imagined elder brothers and three imagined elder sisters and an imagined father and an imagined mother who love each other even more than Martin Landau and Barbara Bain love each other on TV. And some nights, I would SPLIT back to be with Mian, and I would die like she did, and we would play like we used to, and I would tell her jokes and watch her shut her eyes, and her mouth would open from eyebrow to eyebrow, and her chuckles would roll out of her lungs in parcels of wind tickling the armpits of many rainbows, she was like a girl Peter Pan in pink. When Other-Grandma, the Godzilla, incited fights between Pa and Mama, I would SPLIT to spit at Godzilla's face and a fire tiger would fly to the scene, what a fierce eater it was—it would curry her and then eat her every lash, every bone, every finger, every inch of gut, and digest her in pure tiger stomach hydrogen sulfuric bliss. And strangest of all, I could smell all smells thirty notches sharper in the worlds to which I SPLIT. But in the world in which one breathed *real* air, ate *real* food, farted *real* farts, spat *real* spit, sweated *real* sweat, made *real* noise, gesture, waste, posture, and experienced *real* consequences and *real* non sequiturs, my sense of smell was always blunt, and I was never a decadent long-legged anything waiting for men's kissing, indeed I was always the Class Monitor, the Prefect, the model student, the first girl in A class, well-behaved, polite, trying my best to be good and well-liked, for it was the only way to secure Mama's standing in Kinta House. You see, the Kinta people dared not look down too much if your child was ranked number one in the only school in town, although I had overheard them whisper: Too bad her smart child is a girl, her son has a slow tongue, and her small daughter drowned several years ago in a tapioca well.

But since working for E.D.I. Friday, I've ceased to SPLIT at night, as though I've forgotten how to soften my body and let go of my eyes. And I find I dive pencil-straight into zombie sleep and grind my teeth every night, for daytime is made up of suffocating coils of phone calls, emails, deadlines belly-lapping one another. In fright, I begin taking yoga classes to nurture the torque of my spiritual mind lost to the daily pressure of re-defining and re-positioning Every Day Is Friday in the global economics of casual dining and Americana.

And here I am, in limbo and airborne, having said good-bye to Japan, now en route to Singapore, a country where bubble gum is declared a *perennial nuisance* by the Book of Law and therefore illegal to manufacture, import, or buy. Some pity the Singaporeans, for they live in a country too nuisance-free, too clean, too precise, too error-free, too odor-free, too punctual, they say the Singaporean government has failed to see that it is in humans' daily dealings with errors and odors that we see humanity.

Yogi Butman is back to remind me that I must relax my mind. First, he says, don't irk or be irked, try letting come and go the scent of air freshener and the humming sound of the plane. Next, let come and go the sound and scent of the passengers. Let all of them come through and leave your mind, he says. I heed his advice. I take a deep Ujjayi breath. I am feeling my Ujjayi breath fill every sinus cavity in my head. The soothing voice of Yogi Butman is a soft-winged seed sitting in Padmasana three inches above my nose. Yogi Butman utters from his *dan tian*: The Dead Pose is a supine relaxing pose. Haa. Inhale. Saa. Exhale.

H a a. I inhale.

S a a. I exhale.

H a a.

S a a.

H a a.

This is how I summon my calm.

Tranquil in Dead Pose, I sense the awakening clarity of my *chi*.

Haa. Saa.

H a a.

And I hear a man whispering, "... And I peed onto her small leather-clad body ... and ... and ... I felt a fierce surge of jubilation, I felt like singing loudly, but I didn't sing ... instead I whistled, ... without thinking I whistled, for a while I whistled, then I realized I was whistling The Star-Spangled Banner!"

Someone bellows, "Jesus, Dick, did you really?"

"I don't know what overcame me, Mo. I left the joint rather quickly after that."

I open my eyes. No one is sitting next to me. Across the aisle, a man, 2C, clad in black jeans and a beef-red button-down shirt, his BlackBerry in his hand, turns to look at me to make sure I haven't heard him. Our eyes meet. He lowers his head and turns to the man sitting next to him and whispers, "Shit, Mo, I think the woman across the aisle heard me."

Mo, in a white dress shirt, tie-less, tilts his head slightly forward to peek at me. Mo gives me a frown. I frown back.

Mo mutters to his friend, "I don't think she heard anything."

I close my eyes trying to find the soft-winged seed in between my brows. But now inside my closed eyes, I see 2C paying to pee on some women in Tokyo's Ikebukuro District. I see him ordering the service, "*Sumimasen,* a leather woman *kudasai.*" And I hear Mo muttering to Dick, "... and I bet you the leather she wears is synthetic leather. Imagine the cost of having the girls wear cowhide every time a leather girl is ordered. What do you think their margin is? Fifty? Eighty? The cost for girls must be cheaper than the cost of renting that hole in Ikebukuro by at least three times."

And I see Mo and Dick having dinner at the tiny sushi restaurant where unclad girls work as tables. I photographed one of the *nyotaimori* girls. She looked like she was breathless, breathlessly angry, not breathlessly sad, still like a scream held back in the mouth of the dead.

And then I see Mo and Dick and their wives and kids at an E.D.I. Friday in Oklahoma City, gnawing on buffalo wings surrounded by tall glasses of super sundae special mottled with jelly beans.

A churn of airline-port, airline-V8, and airline-peanuts rises to stir at the head of my tongue.

From his Lotus Pose three inches above my nose, Yogi Butman intervenes to help me concentrate: Choose, choose an object for your mind to rest on, choose a half opened rose, and shed and lose your sense of self into the rose. Haa. Inhale. Saa. Exhale.

H a a. I inhale.

S a a. I exhale.

I haven't the time to choose an object when I begin to

see a finger, possibly index, tipped with a tiny piece of contact lens. Then, I see the finger's slow metamorphosis into a man's one-eyed snake wearing a single contact lens. The image of a near-sighted one-eyed snake sends a tickle through my sedentary body. Haa. Saa. Haa. I feel like laughing.

Yogi Butman is back to advise: Nin, you can choose whatever you like as a focal point for your mind's eye, but it is best to choose objects such as a budding orchid or a half opened rose.

Why can't I choose a contact-lensed one-eyed snake? I ask.

Because snakes eat dust, Yogi Butman answers curtly. Because snakes are cursed with the instinct to puncture the faces of gardens and slither through the holes they puncture.

But don't you think a half opened rose, full of potential and beauty, is too Hallmark, too Thomas Kinkade? I ask.

Choose a half opened can of tuna fish then. Yogi Butman is a little irked.

Okay, let me start over, I say.

Haa. Saa. Haa. I see a half opened mouth, lip-balmed.

Yogi Butman murmurs something inaudible under his furry mustache.

The half opened mouth looks like a tight fruit open and broken in the center—o, without words, thoughts, screams, songs, or half chewed food. Then I see her hand stiff at the wrist but soft at the balls of fingers pink from rubbing men's minds craving to know/eat/annex the black inside her elongated o opening. Then I see her face before her fruit breaks—a flower, a nature, fickle, freckled, dim, adazzle, her hair billows of clouds, brows small hills, eyes lakes, cheeks moons, her mouth a breakable fruit, as Chinese poets have long perceived landscape, facescape, desirescape. Then I see a snake, one-eyed and contact-lensed, poking its head gently at her unopened face. Her mouth unopened, she tells the snake in silence: Stop, I must go now, I mustn't be sitting on your bed. The snake pauses and replies in silence: We don't have to sit down, we can stand, don't be scared, once your fruit is broken, your nose is opened.

Yogi Butman interrupts: Hmm, excuse me, Nin, these images are far from peace inducing. You may want to try . . . I turn Yogi Butman off.

No, he didn't say *broken*. He said, once your fruit is touched, your nose is opened. That's what he said. He is no snake. He is a man with a gentle heart. I call him the Locksmith of My Nose.

He was a friend of Frank whom Lara had met at a Tufts University bash a week before spring break in our sophomore year. I agreed to go on the double date because it was the beginning of spring break and the campus was empty but for a few foreign students, and despite Lara's constant prodding, I had not dated ever. I hadn't dated because as part of the college work-study financial aid I received, I had spent holidays and weekends checking in and out reserved materials at the library and flipping burgers at the student center. So I went. The double date began with a northern style dim sum lunch at the overcrowded Mary Chung on Mass Ave. We sat by the window. He was late. He arrived precisely when the scallion pancakes and *dan dan* noodles arrived. He said he got held up and apologized. Frank stood up to give him a bear hug. Lara said hello with a thin wedge of scallion pancake in her hand, she held it like a slim and elegant cigarette. I was tongue-tied. His eyes gentle like water, his jaw pensive, and his earlobes large as Cerignola olives.

We spent the rest of lunch talking about food, Clinton, WTO, lab mice, Clarence Thomas, Tao, death, Suzanne Vega, Alanis Morissette, Aphrodite, pheromones, and aphrodisiacs. The conversation had flowed smoothly until I spoke. Thrice I spoke. No, four times. The first was when the conversation had turned to frog legs, oysters, and bull penis as aphrodisiacs. Lara and Frank were speculating on how a bull penis can best be prepared and served. Without much thought I interrupted to share that I have had, once and only once, in my hometown Kinta in Malaysia, a bowl of spicy bull penis noodle soup, it tasted like *tom yam* beef stew. Everyone was quiet for seemingly thirty seconds or more. He was the first to break the silence, he said he thought a bull's private is for enhancing the men's organ not the women's. Precisely, I replied, feeling utterly lousy about having shared the story, it was a prank of a wicked friend, I said, anyhow it explained why my handshake is often described as manly, I think the bull's balls had gone to enhance the shake of my hand. The laugh was so abrupt— Lara choked and had scallion bits inside her nose.

Then somehow the conversation turned to lab mice. Frank had recently learned from a friend that a preliminary scientific experiment has shown that if a male mouse and a female mouse mate more than eight times in the first twenty-four hours of their first meeting, they will bond for life, otherwise, they will never bond. Lara exclaimed, that's plenty of fucking for a day! Frank said, supposedly, twenty-four hours mouse time is three months human time. Sincerely I meant to quip along the line of—once a week is very human, isn't it? But instead I said: Once a week is very seldom indeed. Again, no one uttered a sound for about thirty seconds. Even Lara pretended not to have heard me. Frank coughed two, three blockish coughs. As for him, I avoided his gentle looking.

The third conversation stopper came when again Frank was telling us about how he has never smelled in his dreams until a recent dream of him eating pungent mashed caterpillars on tortilla chips. Lara asked if he was sure it wasn't mashed avocado, and I chipped in to tell that I have often smelled in my dream, in fact, my nose works the best when I dream or half dream, whereas in real life my sense of smell is somewhat impaired. Like now, I can't smell much of the scallion pie or the *dan dan* noodles, I said, but my taste buds are well, I can taste the pie and the noodles fine. He looked at me with a warm and curious smile on his face. Frank arched one of his eyebrows. Lara wore the Medusa face she got whenever she was about to begin her pontification. Again, the silence seemed as long as thirty seconds or more. But before Lara had a chance to pontificate, he tilted closer to me and said, my sister was like you, Nin, she couldn't sense smells too well until she got married, and then her nose just turned normal, it was like she got her nose back overnight. Good God, Frank could not believe it, while Lara gave me a mischievous glance. Then he raised his teacup and declared: To strange noses in the world. We laughed and raised our teacups and toasted to strange noses. I asked where his sister is now. Without skipping a beat he said she died in a car accident two years before and her husband was killed as well. A just resuscitated conversation dropped dead. Lara whispered a sorry. Frank took a sip of his tea and gave his friend's back a soft pat. I looked at him in disbelief. This time no one spoke for seemingly thirty minutes. Then he smiled and said he was fine, he said he was fine to Lara's *sorry* and Frank's pat, but he was looking at me.

That was our first hour. After lunch, Frank and Lara went their own way. He asked if I cared to take a walk along the Charles River. I nodded. We took the T to Kendall Square and started our walk at Longfellow Bridge. I don't remember much of the walk, except that we didn't talk much, we just walked. Along Memorial Drive we walked. For hours we walked. And the evening arrived quite suddenly. And quite suddenly I found myself sitting on his bed in his studio apartment on Cambridge Street, scared happy, not scared angry or scared upset. But scared nonetheless. For his hands had just landed gently on my bare breasts. "Stop," I said. "I must go now. I mustn't be sitting on your bed."

He dropped his hands. I saw sadness and kindness pool in his eyes. He whispered, "I am sorry. I got carried away . . . I have wanted to touch you . . . all day . . . Nin . . . I . . . I am terribly sorry . . . don't be scared, I won't do anything you don't want . . . and we don't have to sit down. We can stand."

He gave me his hand. We rose together. When we finally stood straight and face-to-face, my back against the cold wall, I was as tall as his chin. Strong chin he has. As he bent down to grab a flannel throw from the bed, the wind his body stirred brushed very slightly the tips of my breasts. I quivered. The familiar numbing joy of my girlish acrobatic fantasy ran through my body. "Please," I said. He gently wrapped the soft throw around my back and shoulders and chest. "Touch me," I said. He hesitated. Then he bent down to kiss, very gently, around my mouth, neck. Slowly he kissed. By the time he got to my ear, he whispered, "Don't be scared, once your fruit is touched, your nose is opened." He moved his hand to where the circus man had gone time after time to place a candy in my girlish fantasies. I held his arm with both hands. I moved to the rhythm of his hand. Joy ruptured and spread from where skin and skin touched. But I felt ashamed, acridly ashamed. I couldn't stop my moving and his looking. Shameless woman I am, I thought to myself, as I rubbed more and more violently against the base of his thumb. And I could smell distinctly the subtle sweetness of his skin—a curious mix of cumin, apple, jasmine. There were tears in his kind eyes—they seemed to be saying: It's okay, Nin, it's okay, I understand, you can let go, you are safe here. Inside the black of his parted mouth, I saw a Small Me, nineteen years of age, mouth opened, dizzy, legs slightly spread, standing riding his hand, the bull hand of a man.

He was Mahar. Mahar Ramakrishnan. The locksmith of my nose. We were bonded for life in three months, human time.

Haa.

Saa.

Haa.

chapter 9

WING: *Mirror*

In Singapore

I was born four times. Tonight is the last of the four, and it happens in Singapore.

The first birth was choice-less, in Vermont. It was 1970. My Irish mother, a hair dresser at Alger in Boston, had gotten pregnant by a Harvard hippie from Hartford, Connecticut, who claimed to be one of the descendants of Yung Wing, the first Chinese to graduate from an American university—Yale, in 1854. According to Mom years later, no one cared enough about his Yung Wing connection to believe or not believe him. But when high, he would burst into eloquent stories of his exotic ancestors. Mom said he had told her that he studied Eastern Civilizations. Well, that helps explain the eloquence, I said. Mom also said that when she met him, he had just broken up with his girlfriend from Hong Kong. Rice King in rebound, I said. Despite the Yung Wing claim, Mom said that he only looked Chinese to her whenever they ate in a Chinese restaurant. He only looked Chinese holding chopsticks, eating from a bowl, ordering food in Mandarin, and surrounded by Chinese waiters and Chinese deco. Well, that explains why, when I am on consulting projects in China, people say I look a little Chinese, and when I am on projects in Korea, people say I look a little Korean. I remember Mom burst into laughter at what I said. But I know she was glad that I resembled her. According to Mom, my face is, in every sense of the word, Celtic. But your size, Mom said, gladly, is surely Chinese. It is a perfect combination, she said, a Celtic face and a Chinese slenderness. Anyway, he died in bed at the peak of a carnal ecstasy, Mom pinned underneath. He had a berry aneurysm. In short a body too tight for too much pleasure of the flesh. Mom moved back to Vermont, where Grandpa and Grandma lived in a small log house twenty girl-steps from the southern bank of Echo Lake. There, she gave birth to my twin sister and me, exactly eight months and eighteen days after his death. Mom named me Wing and my sister Yung, in memory of my father's possible Yung Wing linkage. My father's family name was Cox. My mother's family name was Joyce. I was born Wing Joyce and my sister Yung Joyce.

I was again choice-less-ly born the second time when I was nine. Again, in Vermont. My twin sister had managed to pick the lock of the drawer in which a pistol had been kept. My grandpa's oily pistol stretched across her small palm. We touched it as though it were the tightly feathered skin of a very angry crow. Russian Roulette, she said, let's play Russian Roulette. It was a game we had witnessed in a TV show called *The Wild Wild West.* Stronger, braver, and left-handed, she pointed the pistol at her left temple. We felt our power combined. We paused for seconds. We smiled. The water closet was tiny. We were chest to chest. Half to half. Hero to hero. In *Wild Wild West.* She pulled the trigger. For years, remembering back, seeing every detail come alive, I heard and saw the first and only click of the pistol send a small shadow swimming across my sister's forehead. She looked as though she could not understand the essence of Russian Roulette; how could it be a one-shot game? She looked as though she thought she could stop the bullet from traveling farther to the other side of her head. I saw the bullet-shaped lump stop above her right brow, at the peak of her hill-like brow. Her right eye turned white. I saw a gray and small me in her eye-white. Silence and bullet stood still for as long as we could hold our breath. But always the weaker one, I accidentally let go of my breath. Out was a metallic bullet on the other side of my sister's head. It was chased by a fat column of red. A tiny river of hot red ran down from between my thighs.

I became a woman that spring morning when I was nine, when my stronger and braver half died, when my stronger and braver half became mine. Me. I.

I don't remember much of the days leading up to the funeral, only Mom's voice echoing in the still of the funeral hall.

Mom said: It's not your fault, Wing, the fault lies with God, it's not your fault. In fact Mom whispered at my ear these same words every night for moons and moons after my sister was laid to rest under a maple with berry bushes nearby.

No one knew, as I stood in the water closet watching droplets of water growing fat and elongating at the tip of the leaky tap, with my sister's partial head resting on my shoulder, I could hear her whisper into my ears: Fly, forget the line between you and I. When a droplet grew to its fattest, I could see a tiny twisted pair of us, in red. Fly, she said, forget the line. It was the very last time we stood chest to chest, sister to sister, half to half, for in the course of those silent hours in the water closet, as our blood turned rustier and rustier, I came to learn to ignore the line. I also came to learn how to fly.

But flying is not just a state of mind. It requires faculties. That is if you want to *really*, I mean physically and corporeally, fly.

I have had no problem flying in my mind.

But against a *real* and adult sky, my wings were too small to lift and flutter in the wind.

This is why. It was a sticky day in the summer of 1987. The summer of Oliver North and Iran-Contra. In the lounge waiting to see a gynecologist for the first time, I could not take my eyes away from a man, baseball-capped, who could not move his eyes away from the TV screen. He was with a wife-looking woman. He was cheering to every line uttered by

Ollie as though he were cheering for the Giants or the Mets. From between his tightly controlled lips, you could hear his tightly controlled pride. Yes, you get them, man, you get them, right on, man, right on. Democracy. America is for democracy. America stands for the good. We are against the evil. Evil. His wife's downcast eyes lifted to offer the room a silent apology. Anyhow, my name was called and upon the elevated seat cornered in a small room I was told that my excruciating period, which I had endured for years, was caused by the size of my hymen. My gynecologist said, you have the vagina of a seven-year-old, your hymen is half the size of the tip of a pinky, she said, showing me her pinky, you will need an operation to snip it, you know, like cutting a functional opening, otherwise, it will be unbearable. Do you understand what I am saying, Wing, unbearable, she said. Unbearable. Now, that instantly explained my break-up with John Miller, my high school sugar of two years. You see, the summer of 1987 was my summer between high school and college. Earlier in the spring I had boxed John Miller in the jaw in reflex when he tried to penetrate me per my consent. He almost bit his tongue in half. Well, for my sake, imagine someone pushing a watermelon up your nostril to your brain. John Miller broke up with me in a week. And for all the months leading up to the appointment with the gynecologist, I thought I was a lesbian, and for months I was acting lesbianish. Now that I know, I said to my gynecologist, I think I should find me a man whose penis is small enough to fit. My gynecologist made a cough-like laugh. I thought of John Miller's best friends, Paul and Brendon, who named their penises, respectively, Winston and Salem. The size and the image of a cigarette has been for me a source of mirth ever since. I had my first cigarette that day. The summer day of 1987 was a very Dalí day indeed. It was a day of Salem and Winston and Oliver North and conspiracy and good and evil and a small piece of skin. My skin. It was a day in which I also thought of the rumor John Miller had begun in the months when I was acting lesbianish. He told, via umpteen veins of vines, that I am a *lip.* A new slang word was created by John Miller who did go on to win the poetry prize at our high school graduation. *Lip,* he said. Singular. Not Plural. As in a mouth without an opening. As in a mouth in the form of one big lip.

A few years later, at Stanford, the semester before I graduated, in my Chinese poetry class, as Professor Egan was reciting an A.D. 1000 poem about the peach-like mouth of an empress and how her peach breaks when she sings, I sat in quiet bliss thinking about John Miller and *lip* and the Dalí summer day, and how John Miller had no idea how sexy his rumor and my knowledge of others knowing of my *lip* had made me feel, and how *real* flying requires a functional orifice, and how one month after that summer day, I successfully persuaded Mom to spend two thousand bucks in the breaking of my peach. I treated the entire outpatient surgery sacredly. It was after all the unlocking of my born chastity belt. I was also thinking about how three months after heaven was unsewn with a snip of a thread, I let a man sniff through the slit of my peach. My third birth. At Stanford. I was eighteen.

He was my Professor in Psychology. Keith Brent. The first time he looked at me, he looked as though I were partially dressed. I was not. I was enwrapped in jeans and turtleneck. I returned his looking with a quiet boldness as though I could undress him just as profoundly. Later, my breasts would harden in his looking. And I would wear matching black underwear to see him during office hours. Every week. And I would go in my black miniskirt. And I would always arrive so that I would be the last seen. He leaned over to touch me on my eighth visit. No words were spoken. But I knew it would happen that late afternoon when I walked into his office, for I smelled a piquant smell of roots of spring. He entered my body and became my first wings. I flew, *really*, from between my thighs through my chest, my face, the roof of my head, the trees, the stars, the void, the uncertainties, the unknown beyond the slit until I reached the pure peak. I flew immensely.

But soaked in the fierce smell of berry roots that late afternoon, I knew that the blackberry pleasure, big as the ball of my heel, ebon in body, was not love, true love I mean. I did not care enough for Keith Brent. I opened my body for him because I saw in his body a pleasure I wanted. I saw in his lips a rut I craved. I saw in his strides a man who knows. And I saw us spooning naked in squalls for weeks before that late afternoon. But I did not care enough for Keith Brent. I did not fear losing him. I only wanted a skillful man for my first flying.

After Keith Brent were several catalogs of men. I was driven by skin and only skin. I was letting my skin feast.

But I did not care for the men after Keith Brent.

Until him. Moghai. The managing partner of our Singapore office. His name is Moghai. Until this evening with him. How should I describe him? Three parts water one part fire? We are complementary in nature—he more water, I all fire.

Look at him. He sleeps like an ancient railroad station. Imbued in history and fantasy. In the dim glow of moon and the Singapore nightscape, his brows sit like houses, pensive and honest. We have faxed in our resignation letters this evening. We are leaving for Christmas Island tomorrow. To start anew. New space. New bodies. New eyes. New sense of time. Information-less-ly. Competition-less-ly. Market-less-ly. Face-less-ly. We will build a small house in the migration path of red crabs. We will see love-making reef squids and egg-shooting corals in the surrounding seas. We will plant okra and cook sting-ray okra curry. We will make the sky our blanket and we will spoon underneath it. I can't help thinking about pleasuring him. Repeatedly. Really, linearity is not that relevant. Almost all causes and effects are circular. Essence is what you can't see in the middle of layers of circumferences. Do you see?

Look at me, I am thirty-six. I have had a network of acquaintances and colleagues and clients and men. I am a globetrotting partner at one of the top business consulting firms in the world. I have consumed services. I have been fearless in business. I have also been fierce in pleasuring my eyes my ears my nose my flesh my taste buds. What does it all mean?

Re-allocating wealth and wealth only.

Re-rousing skin and only skin.

I am not afraid of Labor. I am not afraid of Silence. I am not afraid of Insignificance. In fact I often imagine an ideal world a world of anonymity. A world of simplicity. A world of good repeats. A world where neither boredom nor death has the power to drive me.

The key is to follow your skin. Listen to your skin. Let your skin feast. It will open and loosen and lose itself and lead you to the meat, then the bone, then the essence your eyes can't see your words can't limit your mind can't read.

Listen to your skin. Let it breathe. Let it give you the births you need.

Nin

Singapore → Amsterdam

$\mathcal{I}$ am in 3A, a window seat. Behind me, 4A is *a* Russell Crowe. I smile at Russell. Russell sits next to an Asian woman. Possibly Thai. Not only is she Thai, 4B is a stunning Thai with a stunning Thai smile. I give Russell another smile. But Russell is distracted by the shocking body next to him. I have no chance, logistically, facially, bodily, exotically.

Excuse me, miss, may I please have another glass of port?

Is port an after-dinner or a before-dinner drink? Who gives a damn about protocols when no one knows your name? So let there be port and there shall be port.

Port works like a hundred tiny drunken hot-blooded sea snakes swimming away from my mouth toward my neck, stomach, limbs.

Look. Outside the airplane window, against the dark void, Russell Crowe is nibbling on something. Holy smokey, there are two Russell Crowes in my vicinity. I must be more than tipsy. One Russell is sitting behind me, while one is outside the plane window to the left of me. I squint my tipsy eyes and stare close against the window. It looks like the Window Russell is nibbling on a toe. I move my body away from the window. Still, why isn't a Russell Crowe sitting next to me, conveniently available? But I am not available. I am married. I am married to Mahar, Mahar Ramakrishnan. I am not consequence-less-ly carefree. Still, why isn't Russell a 3B? The real 3B is *a* George Costanza. His college-ringed finger is tapping. Tapping to some fragmented thoughts. I turn to look at George's face. He gives a grin. Oh, don't. Let it be known, my principle is this: When I am drunk, I am vain, and I am not talking to anyone except Russell Crowe. But the gate is open, too late to run.

"I see you didn't eat your curry prawn dinner, too spicy?" George Costanza asks.

I burp conspicuously and struggle to will my port-fed lips to form a small please-don't-talk-to-me smile. But I manage to make only a meaningless twitch.

His ringed finger begins to tap again. TapTap. TapTap. George is thinking: How to fire up a conversation between a man and a woman?

"I'm on business." George has his adamant streak. "I was in Singapore attending the largest lingerie convention in the world. I was there to scout the new trends in Oriental women's lingerie. I'm a buyer for several big stores back in the States."

In *Seinfeld*, George's father once had an idea of making bras for older men.

I say nothing. I see his stocky fingers begin to hop to some dissonant rhapsody. Winking winking, his ring is awfully big. Its big band supports its big yellow stone. TAPwink. TAPwink.

I imagine George's clammy fingers, one prominently ringed, kneading my breast.

Holy Monkey. I turn toward the window, head smacking the glass.

"Are you all right?" George asks, his fingers on my elbow.

"Uh-huh." I refuse to turn my head.

"Let me take a look at your forehead. It was quite a bang." George tries to turn my head. His moist fingers touch my temple, his hands blocking my vision.

I close my eyes. I see his thumbs pressing my nipples.

Holy Mega Monkey. I open my eyes.

His concerned face is five inches away. Even the bits of sweat on the tip of his nose and forehead look concerned. He has a wide face. Peculiar and wide. His wet nose is nudging my breast.

Holy Holy Mega Monkeys. Stop. I shut my eyes. I shake his nose and fingers and monkeys off.

George says, "I am sorry. Are you all right?"

All right . . . all right . . . George's *all right* echoes outside my eyes to my right. Like a two-frog antiphony, *all——right all——*

right, backforth backforth, at zero-sum low speed. Russell Crowe too is uttering *all r . . . all r . . . all r . . .* outside the window to my left. A different kind of *all right.* A mouthful *all right.* Hungry and stuffed at the same time.

I shift to center my body neither left nor right. Can Be bad, I am not opening my eyes until the plane lands in Amsterdam.

Mama used to tell me that tiger has many kinds. You can be a good one. She didn't say you are a good one. She said I can be a good one.

And she was right. I *can be* good, but I am not, for I made Mian big when she was only five, and she died. A dead Mian, mouth choked with white tapioca mud, is always at the corner of my eye. Always. I want to forget Mian so bad, but when I begin to forget, I try to remember her by all means. And Mama had X-ray eyes, she could tell when I began to forget. And she would set me straight.

But Mama was right. I am not a good one. I can be a good one.

Can Be is dangerous and can be bad.

I feel it, Can Be is turning into Am Bad.

What's your name?

"I, Am Bad."

"What did you say?" George Costanza is concerned. "Do you need a barf bag?"

I ignore George. Because a new and buoyant voice is now

fluttering underneath my eyelids. A woman's Man Voice. She says: You must sleep your monkeys off, Nin. Thank God you half-sleep when you are drunk. You know one glass of port is enough to give you the happy buzz you like. But no, you had to have five. Airline serving glasses are deceiving, didn't you know that? You are never like this. This irresponsible. This careless. This drunk! What's with you, Nin!

Who are you? I inquire through the slivers of my eyes. Miss Saks, is that you?

Miss Saks, my high school discipline mistress, still has her signature stare of a man. The stare of death. The stare of Alan Rickman. I have seen her staring the truth out of my friend, Lai. In less than eighteen seconds to be precise.

Long time no see, Miss Saks, I heard you finally, officially, no, I mean openly, hitched Miss Lilian Lu. Is that true? What's she like in bed?

Miss Lilian Lu was my Form One English teacher. She made English as easy as Chinese. I loved her.

Miss Saks is not pleased. I see Miss Saks's eyes turn molten-glass-orange inside my eyelids. I feel the heat.

Shut up and sleep! Miss Saks bellows. Stop fluttering your lashes, Nin! How dare you make Russell Crowe suck your toe! He's gnawing on your toe, Nin. Your toe! How dare you enliven your private thought to such an extent when you are sitting in a public plane? You think I don't know why you flutter your lashes? You are bad. All the time. I see through your mind.

You are thinking sex feeling sex seeing sex all the time. I am gonna nail your eyelids dead. Dead. Sleep. Sleep off your monkeys. Sleep off the drunken snakes in your body. Sleep!

But thoughts are not actions, I try to object. Fantasies never impinge. Fantasies are what one does when one can't act on one's fancies. Plus, fantasy is the best of pleasures ... I am quoting Flaubert or Voltaire or someone French. And that's why I can't stop fluttering ... fantasizing ... fluttering my eyelids, Miss Saks.

But I think I manage only to murmur the last of the long sentence "S a k s ..."

"Sorry, what did you say?" George Costanza is less than two feet away. "Are you *sick*? Do you want to throw up or something?"

Did George just say *Wing*?

Wing Joyce, the gorgeous woman, who claimed to be one part Chinese and many parts Irish, who stayed next door to me at the Singapore Marriott, told me about how beef tripe soup can cure a hangover like a magic wand. I photographed her, her beauty was carnal, irresistible. But I doubt they carry tripe soup on commercial airlines. I guess I will have to calm the drunken snakes in me myself. But I have no flute. Neither do I own a mongoose. I am afraid I may have to turn into the Business Blonde in *Sex, Lies, and Videotape*. She masturbates whenever she travels in a plane. She masturbates to calm her snakes.

Stay very still, Nin! Miss Saks is back to command: Don't you dare touch yourself! You are so damn drunk! Sleep it off! Sleep it off and you will be fine!

But another voice emerges to say: Shine! Shine the biggest shine of your life!

George? No, the voice of 4A! The voice of Russell Crowe! He is speaking, from behind. Russell is speaking, phantasmagorically, to the stunning Thai sitting next to him. "I love Asian culture. Your culture is great. I have a theory about it. Like your painting, all the women are clothed, and their bodies are hidden. Whereas in the west, nude paintings are everywhere. My theory is this: Each human is born with a fixed amount of sexual energy waiting to be released. Your people release it in bed. My people release it on painting and sculptures . . ."

What kind of nonsense is that?

Russell, possibly as smashed as I am, carries on. "See what I mean? Like the whole sex thing with Bill Clinton. Let me tell you, the only president who had no mistress and who was totally loyal to his wife was Nixon. But Nixon was the cruelest president in the history of the United States. He could use some Monica, if you know what I mean. Bill Clinton is great. He is at peace. He is for peace. He is confident, decent, thoughtful. He has no monkeys running in his head."

Confident.

Decent.

Thoughtful.

My boss, Rob Campbell, is such a man.

Rob Campbell called me on January 2, two days before my big trip. Two days before I was to leave Mahar and my home in San Diego for my FireWife photo project.

Nin, he said. I need your help.

I know, he said, this will disrupt your travel plans and your photo project. But we are suddenly heating up in the site-negotiations for our Fridays in Taipei, Bangkok, Tokyo, Singapore, and Amsterdam. I need your help, Nin. You are all I got for these international negotiations. Plus, I figure the cities are sort of on your way.

On your way, he said. Confident. Decent.

I bellowed. Silently. My original first stop was Bhutan. Not Taipei!

They are not exactly . . . I said. The image of Al Pacino in *The Godfather* saying *they keep pulling me back in* flashed across my mind.

Nin, I know you are taking half a year off to travel in exotic places on a personal project. I know, Nin. I was the one who approved your leave of absence. I understand its importance, Nin. Didn't you name your project Fire Women or something?

FireWife, I said.

I love the name of your project, Nin.

Rob Campbell likes to say my name.

I only need your help for a few weeks, Nin, he said. Four

weeks tops. Why don't you slightly alter your travel plan and instead begin your photo project in Taipei, and continue it in Bangkok, Tokyo, Singapore, and Amsterdam? I'm confident there are worthy girls and women to be photographed in these cities as well, Nin. Then, I want you to fly back to New York City for the Globalize Friday meeting in early February. After that, I promise, Nin, you can continue your leave without further interruption from me. I promise. See what I mean, Nin?

See what I mean, he said. In pure confidence. Thoughtful. Decent. On January 2. Two days before my big trip.

Sure, Rob. That's why it is January 26 and I am still flying around taking care of E.D.I. Friday business part time. And I have shot only one roll of film so far for my photo essay FireWife. One!

But Rob knew. He knew I couldn't say no. Being dependable, responsible has been my status quo since the day I made Mian big and cock-eyed when she was only five, and she died.

As though reading my mind, Rob Campbell said, So then, you can be guilt-free, Nin, as in you can be totally free to backpack to photograph FireWife, as in you can go seek the meaning of life without interruption from your regular life.

Rob Campbell likes to say *as in, as in, as in,* discursive zoom in, zoom in, zoom in, until one reaches the tiniest truth which is Nothing.

How can Nothing set one free when one is looking for something more?

Nothing is either too small or too big to set one free, if you ask me.

Rob Campbell also likes to say *so then, so then,* linear, simple, easy to grasp.

And of course, *I know, I know.*

I know, Nin, he said.

And I caved, meekly. All right, I said. On January 2.

Great! he said. I look forward to our meeting in New York City. You are my Chief Architect, Nin, I trust your judgment, and I have a hard time keeping up a conversation with your temporary substitute, what's-her-face, Aimee Dubord? She's hyper. She uses critical terms that I don't get and I don't give a damn. For God's sake, tell her the next time you see or talk to her, please tell her that we are in the restaurant business of Every Day Is Friday. We name our drinks Run Rum Run and our dessert Oreo Ooze, and our Friday burger Friday Godsend. Not some sculpted gourmet food for some gourmet magazines for some gourmet modernists or postmodernists. Tell her, the business is a vernacular business. And I am a very vernacular man.

Rob Campbell, the CEO of E.D.I. Friday. It is hard to say no to Rob. It is hard to say no. Period. But I did sort of say *no* to him once when he, a two-year divorced man, standing next to me in an elevator, began stroking my back.

Fuck!

No, I didn't say fuck.

I said I am married. Happily married. To Mahar. Mahar Ramakrishnan. I said, but I am flattered. He stopped his hand. He looked me in the eyes. Confident. Decent. Thoughtful. And then he said, Nin, I am sorry. He paused. It won't happen again. It's just that, no, I mean, I hope I'll find a woman like you, Nin, he said.

The elevator door opened. The In-House Counsel walked in. The conversation turned legal.

The elevator door opened. The In-House Counsel walked out.

The elevator door closed. Rob Campbell turned around and held my face with both his hands. He gave me a confident and thoughtful kiss on the lips. A kiss of the House. I gave his mouth the tip of my tongue. No, I mean I was about to give him the tip of my tongue when the elevator ground to a stop. I peeled myself away from him. No, I mean I peeled myself away from the Tongueful Me and then peeled the Tongueful Me away from the Man of the House.

I was about to give him my tongue. Tongue!

What's wrong with me?

I almost caved and made way for the House. Had it not been for the elevator grinding to a stop, I would have offered the House my whole tongue. And the House would have swallowed it in bliss.

As a woman, can my tongue be eaten seriously and my non-tongue essence still be taken seriously, simultaneously? In a job situation, I mean.

Lara said, sure, I don't see why a woman's tongue can't be crudely and pleasurably sucked and her brain be seriously and respectfully sucked all at the same time. Sure, she said.

No, I said. Plus, I am married.

That's why I steer clear of taking elevators with Rob Campbell. I am not afraid of Rob Campbell. I am more afraid of the Tongueful Me. And frankly, I don't dislike Rob Campbell. He is merely an everyday man with his everyday know-how to be a man, his everyday plan, and his everyday slippage, coping, ego, love, regret. But I do abhor the fact that Rob Campbell thinks that I understand the essence of Friday so very well. As though E.D.I. Friday's Friday is one profound chicken finger and I am the Julia Child of finger foods. And that I can make E.D.I. Friday more Friday than anyone he knows. When there is a crisis involving the meaning of Friday, Rob would say, call my Chief Architect Nin, she can tell you the divine faces of a Friday.

No more. Really. No more Friday is a red-cushioned chair. Friday is red-white red-white red-white. Friday is everything Americana. Friday is a row of Tiffany replicas. Sure, T.G.I. Friday's has sued us for trademark infringement umpteen times. We counter-sued as many times. And everything is as pending as the end of the world. Sue you. Sue me. Sue you back. Sue me back. In the meantime, the lawyers and their hired experts could no longer fit into their pants and offices. I am fed up.

Fed up with corporations obsessed with litigation, competition, globalization, standardization. Standardize number of layers in a layer cake. Number of scoops in a jumbo soup. Number of spittle in a spit. Standardize standards. Standardize standardizing standards. Standardize the way we sit, eat, shit, the way we love and live. Globally. Standardize beauty. The Nicole Kidman standard that is. Standardize happy. Are you Land Rover happy or Range Rover happy? Louis Vuitton happy or Gucci happy? Buy buy buy. Waste waste waste. *How can we claim compassion fatigue when we show no sign of consumption fatigue?* Sebastião Salgado, verbatim. Speed speed speed. Supersonic. Up the hill. Expedite. On the hill. Expedite. Down the hill. Expedite. A foot in the coffin. Expedite.

T. S. Eliot's Prufrock measured out his life with coffee spoons.

How should I measure mine? By the pounds of hamburger meat? Feet of cheese? Number of E.D.I. Fridays in the world? Number of baby spiders eating their own mothers?

Lara constantly reminded me that my job at E.D.I. Friday spawns multinational business organisms born to suck dry differences, ardor, magic, natures, myths, power, local cultures.

Enough!

I heard someone whispering, "Miss, I think she may need some barf bags, please." George Costanza? What is he up to now?

I am fed—ALL THE WAY—up.

I can feel the whole world sitting on my tongue now.

A busy world. A churning, ornate world.

A man-made world where we evaluate, judge, have, not have, do, not do, be, not be, value, mark, pursue, preserve, write, remember, disvalue, unmark, discard, destroy, erase, forget. Skin deep we are. Skin deep.

Skin deep I am. Skin deep.

Origin. Value. Identity.

Origin. Skin. Skin.

We live for the skin, by the skin, of the skin.

Miss Saks, are you still there? I can't feel it. I can't feel the core. My origin. The origin under my skin. My beginning, Miss Saks, I have no perspective of my beginning. My context is too small. I have a nagging feeling that we are way past the optimal, way too cultured, too layered, too masked. Can you honestly say you can feel the very nature our cultures culture?

Can you? Yeah you, whoever you are outside my eyelids.

How can we *feel* and *live* the core?

How? Peel. I must peel.

Peel layer after layer . . . of . . . the calyx of soul.

But is Calyx peelable? Is my original nature inside? Is Fire Me buried in there? Can I live the core without hurting anyone?

Tell me the impact! I roar, gently, verbatim, from my high chair, like Rob Campbell does. Rob Campbell likes to roar: Everything has cost, what is the cost? Not everything has benefit, what is the benefit? I don't care how you do it, just do it!

So, God, Buddha, Allah, Whoever You Are, please, please show me the impact! I roar. Very gently.

Out of some whirlwind. Not very gently. Only God roars back: YOU WANT ME TO SHOW YOU YOUR CORE BY COMMITTING YOUR *REAL* BODY? God has the speaking voice of James Earl Jones and Judi Dench in one body.

Yes! Yes, of course! I am done with dreaming and fantasizing. Done. Please *really* return my Small Me, Fire Me, my nature before accidents and cultures began to work on me, before order and responsibility. Give me back the carefree me, the small and wild me, the core, the coil, the very original coil, loose from the machine.

That's it, God, I want my spring detached from the Machine, the Guilt!

God is not responding.

You made the Machine, didn't you, God?

THE MACHINE? God inquires uproariously.

Are You *too* attached to the Machine? I ask, carefully.

Like a wise Buddha, God offers only a golden lotus silence in return.

Regardless, God, please cut me loose from the Rat Race,

the Machine! The Guilt! Please, God, I've heard of your Strength. I want only my Guiltless Original Me. Please.

Suddenly a LARGER GOD roars out of a larger whirl-wind: HOW DARE YOU TRY TO OPEN THE DOORS OF MY FACE! DO YOU NOT KNOW I AM LEVIATHAN? DO YOU THINK YOU CAN DRAW OUT LEVIATHAN WITH A HOOK? A MERE HOOK. A LESS-THAN-A-HOOK HOOK.

God is angry. I heard he distributes sorrows when he is angry.

Okay. Fine. If I do the cutting loose myself, God, do you suppose, perhaps, doing a Russell Crowe would help? I shout, making myself heard in godly wind.

God is silent for less than eighteen seconds to be precise. Then, he roars a final thunderous roar from afar. Unexpect-edly afar. Detachingly afar.

I quiver.

George Costanza is back to knead my breasts with his hands. Rob Campbell gives me a long kiss on the mouth. But Russell Crowe clamps his fists and boxes the two men off. So, I kiss Russell on the lips, in lust and in gratitude.

Stay still, Nin! A nervous Miss Saks is back with admo-nition and advice: I can't believe you are so drunk! Stay still! You can fancy for all the world in your mind. Just don't spill your fancy over to your *real* fingers, Nin. You are in an airplane full of *real* people. You hear. Stay very still. Stay in books. Stay in films. Stay inside your eyes. Stay in the private corners of your mind. Don't spill. Don't spill and mix realities. Don't make flesh-sin out of dream-sin.

I see Miss Saks turning into Alan Rickman bowing down in front of me to hold my waist. Wow. But just before sharp bliss, I see Mian, my small sister, big and cock-eyed, lost in space, trying to breathe.

I choke. At the moment of ecstasy.

I find myself alone in a raft skinned with barf bags, leaden with white tapioca mud, exiting the calm half of a cerulean sea and entering the stormy half, dirge slow, looking for something, something more.

Am I inside a Magritte painting?

Is the sky about to rain a funny bowler hat rain?

Then I vomit my body inside out.

Out too is a block of guilt, white as tapioca mud.

At the corner of my eye, I see George Costanza ejecting himself from his seat screaming for help.

chapter 11

MARIA: *Mother*

In Amsterdam

$\mathcal{M}$y left one is a non-discriminating, paper-pale prostitute who swells and burns at all contact, I mean all, almost instantaneously. I call her Breast, short for Fire Breast. My right is a righteous, mothering wife; she is steadfast, smaller, creamier in color. I call her Maria.

No one sees, but every morning on the way to my data-entry work, in the teeming tram, I sit with my arms across my breasts, my right palm cupping Breast and my thumb squeezing her head through my dress.

I can't sit any other way. If I don't sit this way, the lurid wind in Breast can grow so amok that it knocks my helpless head against the tram window. So I surrender every morning and feed her the squeeze. I feed her until the tram passes the Damstraat McDonald's, the first stop after which I get off for my data-entry job. But I usually arrive with fifteen extra minutes for a cup of McDonald's coffee. I also arrive early for its complementary chocolate mint wafer, wrapped in shiny green paper, lodged between the coffee cup and the tray.

I detest the wafer. And I abhor the coffee just as much. Together they remind me of my stepfather, who used to lodge me against the wall, his legs half-hanging from my small bed, tart coffee on his breath. He used to insert into my mouth a piece of very minty chocolate sweet afterward.

They say humans need rituals to mark their lives, and life markers to make sense of chaos and hope. They are right. I do my morning ritual to mark something. I think I am marking the horrid Zero in my life, just so that I can begin every day from Zero. You see, from Zero, I can't sink any deeper. I can only rise.

Tendrils of coffee steam rise in front of my eyes. I stare at them. They are dancing a Zero dance. Breast says, drink it. Maria objects from the right. Meanwhile, the cocoa mint is humming. Dancing. Humming. Coffee. And mint. I have no choice but to drink it and swallow it. From Zero I can only rise.

Despite the benefit of Zero, I try. I try to go against the will of Breast. I try to sit like everyone else in the tram, hands resting on the bags on their laps, and I try so hard not to cross the street and enter McDonald's and drink the burnt-semen coffee and follow with a piece of mint cocoa wafer. But I can't can't do it. The ritual is complete when I swallow the complementary cocoa mint wafer. Whole. Without chewing.

Like a Chinese bride at the end of her face-opening ceremony, when her face-hair is plucked clean, I become strangely fresh and confident.

I walk out of the morning McDonald's. Anew.

And I think of the six years during which Mom worked the night shifts. Days consisted of school bus /school /school bus /*goudse* /bread /and yogurt /school work /cooking /dinner /housework /angst /angst /angst and my stepfather's coming into my room shooting his water and giving me one of his minty cocoa candies afterward.

So you see, I have a problem with my lips and the big long hole between them. I leave them lipstick-less. Why highlight them when I am not proud of them? They are like Breast, always longing for something dangerous and bad.

Maria says that my mouth has received sin, that I should learn to reject the coffee and mint. Will, child, will, she says, you can become free only when you will. But Breast complains from the left, I liked his heavy hand touching me, you know, it did please me, it was quite nice when he rubbed me, I want to be fucked again. Maria rolls her eyes at Breast: How could you say such a thing, he molested you, do you understand what that means, he raped you, violated you, idiot.

A picture of a supermodel stands queenly by the telephone booth across the cheese store. I call her Kate Moss, short for all who look like Kate Moss. Kate checks me every morning as I walk the short block from McDonald's to my office. She says: the subtle curls in your hair (check), your subtly lined eyes (check), your breasts, your hips, your neck (check, check, check). But your outfit could use less color; stay with the simple and elegant, Kate says, brown and black, for instance, is a sophisticated combination; yours is not quite there; your blouse is too orange, it is too loud, and its line is not simple enough. And you must work on your inner thighs and tummy; her bean-size navel stares sternly.

Little does she know, in her queenly presence I am tucking in my tummy, two inches toward my back. Imagine an offended Kate Moss leaping out of her gigantic poster frame pointing, squirming, tummy, your tummy, fifty extra pounds of meat is hanging, hanging outside your black pants. I can see it swaying, up, down, up, down when you walk. You know, it looks bad, very bad, you are fat, very very fat. Do you see, do you see, my gosh, how could you let it!

Maria says only Kate Moss can look so queenly in just underwear. But she is not smiling. For all we know, she could have been all wrought up inside in front of the camera man when her queenly shot was taken, a tummy pain, the tummy pain after and before a vomit.

But of course, she could also be the luckiest girl on earth: born this thin, stays this thin, naturally natural and naturally thin. And all her life never thinking twice eating a second bowl of butter pecan ice cream, or taking a third serving of a potato dish, or savoring a slab of blackened steak as big as a plate.

Maria says Kate Moss is a fake created by the camera man. You are *real*. *Real* people eat, and some even enjoy their food. You need food for strength. Food is good, *eet eet eet eet eet.* Breast shivers: please, no food, please, food makes the girl fat, very very fat.

It is half past eight. Most of my colleagues have not arrived for work yet. I place my tote in one of the corners of my cubicle and begin. They call me the Flying Fingers. I can enter data at a velocity approximately seven times quicker than average. Of course my bosses have no idea, after the squeeze in the teeming tram and the coffee and the mint and the screaming Kate Moss, that it is time for Breast to rest and Maria to work. Maria is the pilot behind the flying fingers. She is steadfastly error-free.

When the digital-red twelve-thirty announces lunch break, Breast automatically wakes up from her nap and declares, fuck data entry. Hey Maria, hey data-entry clerk, stop looking so serious like you earn a million bucks a year data-entering, you know, the girl must work on her hanging tummy, I kid you not, it is falling outside her pants. Are you listening, Maria? Hey, don't feed her too big a lunch, do you hear?

But Maria heeds no one.

Breast is very agitated in the eatery. She screams at Maria

and me. Oh Christ, Special Indonesian Lunch Day. The gal behind the counter is wearing a batik cap, no, no, no *babi ketjap*! No *gado-gado* either. Maria, *gado-gado* comes with peanut sauce. Peanut sauce can clog your arteries while pleating your inner thighs instantly. No, *babi ketjap* is as bad. *Babi ketjap* is pork in soy sauce. A small bite of pork meat carries a thousand calories. Why don't you just take a cube of *Leerdammer*? A small cube and two crackers. Drink a lot of water. It is lunch for Christ's sake. You should eat light at lunch. Oh Christ, Maria, shit, I say no *babi ketjap*. What? Plus *erwtensoep*!! Are you out of your mind!

Maria heeds no one.

Despite Maria's willpower, I bow over a toilet bowl half an hour later per the command of Breast. And then I gargle. I thoroughly brush my teeth. They say tummy acid is bad for your teeth. And from my tote I take out a piece of apple and six sticks of celery and four sticks of carrot. And I eat them quickly.

Maria is not pleased. This is the last time, she says, last, last, you can't go on like this. The child will get sick. Can't you see she is already too thin. She needs her food. Meat. Normal food. You stupid bimbo. Idiot!

One-thirty. I am back to my cubicle. Anew.

Five-thirty. Breast is snoring. Maria napping. I am beat. Very very beat. And hungry indeed. It is time to go home.

Outside the tram window, I see a hungry me looking at me.

I left home/my stepfather/the horrid Zero when I was sixteen. Maria was the heroine.

A billboard reads: *Welcome to Amsterdam. Life is a state of mind and tulips and cheese.*

Life is Maria battling Breast.

Maria murmurs in her nap: why don't we try cosmetic surgery, we can get rid of her totally, I mean, from the root up; we have some savings we can use.

Breast twitches in her sleep.

But, I know. I know when I lie in bed tonight, I will dream about dying into nothingness in which there is neither Maria nor Breast. No I, no me, no mine, no state of mind, no hell, no lips, no cocoa mint, no angels, no space cakes, no wedging, no black tulips, no Kate Moss, no next life, no next anything. Zeros will have no meaning. And last but not least, no coffee of any sort, please.

But as I sail into my dream, I know I will first see this— that I will wake up tomorrow morning a Kate Moss. I will wake up naturally natural and naturally thin, and Maria will cease to exist, and Breast will wilt into a torpid piece of meat, and I will have no need to engage in opposites.

But as I sail deeper into my dream, I know I will hear the night-hunger crying in my tummy acid. And my ears will echo: *eet eet eet eet eet.* And my lips will purr seductively: Give me a snake please, your full snake, please, and the mint, yes, the cocoa mint.

But I will ultimately see, inside the dreaming lids of my eyes, my young death waiting. I will see that I will die into nothingness. Utterly. A nothing, neither absent nor present. As I have desired. As I have dreamed. A Nothing.

The gypsy woman in Zeedijk told me, you cannot hurdle over the age of twenty-three. And she refused to take my fee.

N I N

At Amsterdam Schiphol Airport

*D*o you like mountains or oceans?"

"..."

"Do you like mountains or oceans?"

The voice is at once moiling and soothing.

I open my sleepy eyes in slivers. I see no one.

I shut my eyes.

Copying E.D.I. Friday is making me nuts in the head. Nuts. Can't believe I still have one more business meeting to attend in New York City. But, after New York City, there will be no more part time shooting FireWife and part time taking care of Friday's business, like I have done in the past month. After New York City, I'll be full time on FireWife. I draw in a deep breath. After New York City is life. Life.

"Do you like mountains or oceans?"

This voice is intimately distant.

Again I open my eyes in slight slivers.

Who's talking? Where am I? Tokyo? Bangkok?

No, Amsterdam Schiphol International Airport to be precise. I am waiting for my flight to the Big Apple, that's right.

"DO YOU LIKE MOUNTAINS OR OCEANS?"

Under my half open eyelids, I see, across from me, an old man sitting low in his seat as though he's been sitting there for a thousand years.

"DO YOU PREFER MOUNTAINS TO OCEANS?" Again, he bellows. Simply, urgently he bellows.

I sit up from my slouch. "I am sorry . . . ," I say.

"Tell me, do you like mountains or oceans?" Suddenly softer his voice. But he has a pair of stabbing blue eyes. They are tiny knives. The tiny knives of an aged alpha male. The tiny knives of a seventy-year-old Russell Crowe. Not again! Don't worry. I am sober this time. Smashed and vomited on the flight here a week ago was my first and only. Really, I am sober and proper day and night all the time all my life.

"Why do we so extol people who are sober and proper and punctual and polite all the time?" the old man inquires, out of the blue, gentle as a yogi.

Is he telepathic?

"Polite people create the categories of etiquette and normality and civility to glorify the polite, the normal, the civilized, and stigmatize the different," he expounds. "Polite people create the idea of property out of trees, lakes, atolls, meadows, hills. Polite people create the idea of conquer and conquest out of mountain tips. Polite people own. Polite people invent standards, systems, protocols, and legal and moral and economic and political and epistemological and practical and punctual infrastructures and institutions. Polite people fit. Neatly and legally. They are *legit*. Everyone must strive to be *legit*, polite people teach. I was *legit*. But what the fuck for?" He pokes his pinky into his nostril to dig. Offensively. Defensively. Philosophically he digs.

A long philosophical minute digs by. In vain the effort. Thank goodness. But I am digging everything he says.

"MOUNTAINS OR OCEANS?" he demands for like the tenth time. His eyes piercing. Dancing. Searing. Waiting.

"Mountains," I say. Softly. Why did I answer him? Who is he?

"Why mountains?" he demands.

"Because it's close to a pure silence." Surprised at my speedy answer, I'm also surprised that I answered at all. What for?

"Why do you prefer silence?" He raises his eyebrow.

"Because . . . I'm seeking . . ." The idea of seeking seems replete with self-importance. So I try again. "I mean I'm trying to find . . ." What was the question?

"Find what? A whoppy zippo? A nothing?" he asks, as though the world has never been his oyster.

"Well . . . no . . . I'm trying to find a . . . a place . . . that is beyond sounds . . . sounds and colors."

Sounds and colors? *Sheng se.* That is the Chinese part in me rendered in English. I try again in as pure an English language as I can garner. "I am looking for that raw most and truest layer in nature . . . in life . . . in being . . . you know, that layer that is beyond words . . . beyond noise . . . beyond values . . . beyond frills . . . beyond surface . . ."

Who am I to mention "the truest layer beyond surface"? Christ, I spend my life copying and copying E.D.I. Fridays worldwide. And anytime now, he may bellow aloud, LOOKING FOR THE WHOPPY ZIPPO YOU MEAN??? I must preempt him. So I add, an old habit kicks in, "If you know what I mean."

"Beyond surface? Beyond the skin?" He ponders with a pinch of doubt sprinkled over his arched brow.

"But the body must be kept open by the skin," he says.

A shudder runs down the nape of my neck. I feel like eating.

Something.

"And skin *is* the catalyst for the body." He drives home his point.

"What do you mean?" I ask.

Who is this man?

He looks like Shel Silverstein, but not quite. His earlobes big as Roma tomatoes.

He doesn't explain, instead he brings out two small apples from his pocket and hands one to me. "Do you know the apple is the most misunderstood fruit in history? Have an apple instead," he says. He sinks his teeth into his apple, prodding me to follow suit. I sink mine into mine. Wait. Can't believe I just took a big bite of something given by a stranger. Can't believe I actually swallowed the bite of apple. Its unwashed skin strangely saline and spicy. Its juice sweet and sour. The fruitless digging he did a minute ago, yuk! How long has the apple been in his pocket? I try to empty my mind of apples, pockets, fingers, boogers. Needless to say, I stop after the first bite. But I am one bite too late.

A long-legged silence loiters by.

"I love the oceans," he declares in a soft apple voice.

"I love the oceans," he repeats himself without intermission. "Oceans are changes. Oceans are motions. Oceans are movements of nature. Constant change. Changing constant. Whichever. It doesn't matter. Have you felt the oceans before? Have you? Have you FELT THEIR POWER?" He is quick to anger. He speaks as though he's sure and suddenly angry that I haven't felt the oceans. He speaks in defense of oceans. He speaks like a wounded man. All of a sudden.

"Yes. But I don't love the ocean," I answer.

"Why?" His eyes knives. Confused but sharpened.

"Because you can fall off its surface into its substance and suffocate," I say.

I see a glimpse of soft blue in his eyes. Then the blue again hardens into blue knives. His caustic eyes remind me of the young woman, possibly Chinese, whom I photographed just this morning in downtown Amsterdam, who gawked at her cup of McDonald's coffee as though she could ogle out truth, love, justice, beauty.

"You mean you have *never* felt the power of water?" Relentless his pellucid knives.

"Well, anyway," he mutters away, "despite the constant changes in oceans and the changing constant in mountains, still I believe there are two types of human beings on earth—those who thrive on changes versus those who thrive on constant. As in those who love oceans"—he points at himself—"versus those who love mountains"—he points at me, his eyes soft and happy, his grin as biscuit-yellow as his teeth.

"Do you get it?" he asks. "Like the South American Fire Ants versus the Pandas," he explains.

"Ah-chooooo!" he sneezes. Once.

The augury of sneeze. Malaysian Chinese believe that one sneezes because one's name is concurrently spoken somewhere in the world. The louder one's name is spoken the louder one sneezes.

Yes, God is in a constant sneeze. So are Buddha and Allah.

Someone, perhaps as far away as China, is saying his name.

"Your ancestors from China?" he asks, rubbing his nose.

I smile. Telepathy. Mahar's great aunt was telepathic.

"Yes, but I was born and raised in Malaysia. Malaysian born and raised Chinese American to be exact," I reply. The idea of me an unauthentic Chinese crosses my mind.

"I know of your diasporic kind," he says. "The once or twice or thrice transplanted people. Born one place. Raised one place. Cultural Motherland one place. Citizen of yet another place. You have no sense of *land.* You feel as though you belong to everywhere and therefore nowhere at all. An eternal foreigner, aren't you?"

Who is he? He understands me and the conditioning of my being.

But I do have a sense of land. My memory is my land.

"Show me your right hand!" the old man commands. Abruptly. Perfunctorily.

"What? Why?" A glimpse of a two-legged cat in a Boston Chinatown alley flickers at the corner of my eye. I am not having my fate read again.

"You must," the old man has the temerity to insist.

"Do you see the future or the past?" I ask, not offering my hand.

"I see only the buried, the hidden, the unconscious cognition," he replies. "And I can free your future from your past."

Intrigued, I show him my palm.

"What's up with your pinky?" he right away asks.

Shit!

"What's up with your pinky?" he asks again.

"I . . . cut it . . ."

"When?"

". . . first year in college . . ."

"Why?"

"Because . . . I was beginning to forget my sister . . . I wanted . . . I mean I needed . . . a reminder of the pain I had caused my family," I whisper.

His eyes turn Buddha blue, as though he completely understands my woe, my guilt, my need to remember, and my equal need to forget. Then he closes his eyes and begins to draw invisible circles with his index finger about an inch above the core of my palm. The circles feel like a widening river churning in clockwise twirls.

Is this some voodoo magic? Will I turn into an earwig? I am scared. The river vanishes.

"Don't worry. You'll see," the old man comforts. Convincingly.

I soften my body. The river returns. I close my eyes. Inside my eyes, I see my booted feet. I am standing in the kitchen of my home in San Diego. Mahar asks me to leave my boots on. He presses his front against my back. I see Mahar's brown hand against our kitchen window. Mahar has a sweet scent. He is not musky. Can a man be sweet and musky at the same time? I feel Mahar's other hand stiffening and stiffening on my tummy. Miss Saks says I am sick in the head. She says I have not the chance to live the monkeys in my head. She says

I must deal with the long-locked monkeys first before I can really settle down to love softly, longly, deeply. She tells me to unleash my monkeys in the worlds of books, movies, fantasies, TV. Mahar is cooking me a dinner now. He moves about the kitchen like a body of sweet water swirling by the rocks, the chopping block, the island, the fridge. I look out the kitchen window. I see another me sitting in an airplane, hungry. And this other me is in awe. Awe. Because the man sitting next to me, a stranger, has just placed his hand on my thigh. I quiver. I turn to look at him. He has a wing-tipped upper lip. Our eyes lock our bodies in a cabin up a hill by a seasonal stream for hundreds of seasons. He enters me season after season as though time has no standing in our imaginings.

"Who is the stranger?" an old voice asks, from far away.

"I am not sure," I say. Weakly. Eyes shut. What I didn't say is: I have seen him before, in the private corner of my mind, I have seen him there many times, he has a wing-tipped upper lip, sometimes I call him Russell Crowe.

"He is the musky fire you want," the old man says nonchalantly.

I shudder. The river vanishes.

I open my eyes.

"Don't open your eyes! I am not done!!!" the old man shouts.

"But I am," I say, meekly, retrieving my hand, feeling the heat of Russell Crowe. Russell is four parts fire. Mahar is a night river swelling to a Chopin nocturne. Is Mahar four parts water, or lava base, three parts water one part fire?

The old man shakes his head slightly. "That's what we are put here to do," he says. "To want water. Want fire. Pursue water when we have fire. Pursue fire when we have water. We're put here to want, have, begin to neglect what we have and want something else, want, have, begin to neglect what we have and want something else, vacillate, oscillate, back forth back forth between stable and familiar bases and new and exciting places. We are put here to struggle. To suffer."

"It's like wanting cherry and having egg, having cherry and wanting egg."

He pauses for cherries and eggs to take shape in my mind's eye.

Then he says, "The cherry part in us longs for flight, thrill, surprise, uplift. The egg part in us gravitates toward safe landing, stable surface, order. We swing from wanting cherries to wanting eggs to wanting cherries. Swing. Swing. The larger the swing the larger the pain. The larger the pain the larger the pleasure. The larger the pain and pleasure the larger the need to seek equilibrium. The economics of negotiating these mini equilibriums is everyday and endless," he enlightens. "Like my hands, for instance, my left hand is excitatory, my right inhibitory, when I clasp them together, they feel like my penis, a splendid house of excitatory and inhibitory forces."

He presses his hands together.

I must have frowned.

"Have doubts?" He raises his brows. "Let me quote you *Scientific American.* Almost verbatim. Quote. Within the penis, and throughout the nervous system, a man's sexual response reflects a dynamic balance between EX-CI-TA-TORY and IN-HI-BI-TORY forces. Whereas the sympathetic nervous system tends to inhibit erections, the parasympathetic nervous system is an important excitatory pathway. Per the command of the medial preoptic area of our brain ... hmm ... I've forgotten the rest ... I'll stop here. End quote. But you get the gist." He inflates his cupped hands to the size of a cantaloupe.

Had he continued, I would have blurted out—spare me the details. Please.

"You," he says, "are a hundred eggs looking to become a hundred cherries. Water looking to become Fire. Humans, they vacillate in the deepest nooks of their minds. They vacillate all the time. Egg. Cherry. Egg. Cherry. Egg. Cherry. Egg. Then they breed. Then they deny themselves cherries. Then they die. Egg. Cherry. Egg. Cherry. Egg. Breed. Deny. Die."

Who is this old man inflating and deflating his cupped hands? Who is this man speaking three hundreds miles an hour outside the box of a normal conversation?

"And let me quote the Dalai Lama. Or was it Oprah? Quote. IF THERE IS NO MORAL OBSTACLE, WHERE IS THE VALOR?" The old man shouts out his final insight and nods to his own reckoning.

"Stop fighting, my child." He smiles. "Begin living with the swing. Begin being with things. Let come and go. Let come and go."

Stop fighting what? Let what come and go? Cherry? Egg? Both? And I wonder if there are people who get to eat eggs and cherries simultaneously all the time all their lives.

"What's your name?" I ask, changing not too subtly the direction of the conversation away from his still pumping hands.

"I can't help it, I am Jack."

What can't he help? But good, look, he stops pumping his cupped hands. He extends his hand across the space between us.

I, hollow, hungry, dreamy, give his hand a shake. His hand is warm. It has the coarse and hard surface of a slice of slightly toasted bread.

I love warm, coarse, and hardened hands. And he's not releasing my hand.

"What's your name?" he asks in an almost whisper.

"Nin." I pull my hand firmly out of his. Big Me, Water Me, she is always around pulling my hand firmly out of pleasure she deems risky. Big Me is Egg, not Cherry.

"N. I. N . . . G?" he spells.

"No, N. I. N."

"What does it mean?"

"Harmony. What does Jack mean?"

"Do you want the long version or the short?"

"Give me the short first," I say.

Staring at his open hands, "The short version is this," he says in an abrupt solemnity. "Jack is a woman in the body of a man, Jack understands patterns of any palm, left or right, of any woman or man."

My mouth is dry. Nothing makes sense.

"Do you want a glass of red?" Jack asks.

"Okay," I say. Defense-less-ly. What is happening? Is this some kind of hypnosis? Am I in danger? But why do I feel tranquil and safe? Is Jack insane? Or is Jack a man with a soul long burdened by an imagination running amok? Is he flying to the Big Apple, too?

"Are you flying to New York City, too?" I ask.

"Nah, been there, done that"—Jack doesn't waste a beat—"and you will also *need* some bread." He says *need* as though I am in severe need of new blood, new bone, new flesh.

Why do I *need* some bread?

"Because there are *not* two kinds of eating, my child." He is unmistakenly telepathic! "There are three!" he exclaims. "Eating for nutrients! Eating to satiate a decadent desire! And last but not least, eating for the ritual of starting anew a new leaf! And you, my child, you need the last the most at the moment, you need to eat to expel *completely* the tapioca guilt you have felt for so long. So that you are free to eat cherries when cherries come. So that you can eat eggs in pure peace when eggs return."

Goose bumps creep across my thighs and arms. How does Jack know about tapioca? Does that mean he knows I caused my sister's death when she was only five, I made her big and cock-eyed, and she died?

"Take my hand now. Close your eyes. Make a wish. But don't wish like Lester does," Jack orders.

Who is Lester?

"Lester is the lad who wasted his wishes on wishing. Shel Silverstein, verbatim."

And telepathic Jack gives me his hand. I grip it. Our hands touch like warm river and warm river coalescing. Seamless our touch. Thousand years our touch. Inside the lids of my eyes now, I see Small Me, unclad, sleeping in an egg made of layers of transparent ice sheets. The egg begins to melt under a sky magnanimously pregnant with warm persimmons. As the egg melts, my fingers are waking, then my ears, my soul, then the tip of my nose, my eyes, and in my half dreamy state, I begin to whisper thank you, thank you, Jack, thank you for the release.

When I open my eyes, Jack is gone; in my hand, I see his fading hand changing into a slice of bread.

A solid slice of baguette lies blissfully on my palm.

Hungry, I bring the bread to my mouth and finish it in three bites.

An airline glass of red wine sits on his empty armrest.

I stare at the glass of red for a few moments, wondering what has just happened, but nothing coheres. I reach for the glass. I finish the red in one gulp.

It's hard to say exactly what or how. I feel fresh, I feel like smiling, singing.

I wonder how long this new good strange feeling can last. Or is it the bliss before death. The headline would read: Woman, Malaysian born and raised Chinese American, poisoned by a deranged man at Amsterdam Schiphol Airport terminal, but woman died with a smile.

But I hear the old raspy voice come back to comfort: A hibernation is a covert preparation for a more overt action, *Invisible Man*, Ralph Ellison, almost verbatim.

Jack, is that you? I can't see you. I can only hear you. What's going on?

You have hibernated long enough, Nin. We can't help it. You are waking. You are four parts fire having to live the life of four parts water. This FireWife journey is for you to live the way you are, the way you *truly* are, temporarily.

Temporarily, he says.

Can *Live the way I truly am* hurt someone I love? I ask.

That's why it's temporary, he says. Remember, Nin, long-lasting utopia cannot and does not exist. Utopia is by nature short-lived.

Does that mean I can temporarily live *completely* free from everything?

You can't live free from Everything, Nin, like you said it yourself, how can Nothing set you free if you are looking for Something? Jack is whispering from an ethereal place now.

Unreal. This is like receiving a temporary Almighty Okay to embark on a carefree vacation from one's regular life.

I know, he says, frankly, the others think you deserve only two weeks of TE, but I got you five months, he says.

What's TE? I ask.

Temporary Exile, he says. TE is like a small, short-lived wrinkle on a Super Gel Organismic Universe. In five months, everything will go back to normal.

Everything will go back to normal, he says.

You got it, TE isn't some *paradigm-shift* vacation, Thomas Kuhn, not so verbatim, Jack explains.

The name Thomas Kuhn almost rings a bell. Who is Thomas Kuhn?

Silence.

Who are the others, Jack?

More silence.

Who are you, Jack? Are you an angel looking to get your wings? Are you an angel gone bad? Are you the devil? Or are you a Kitchen God moonlighting as an Airport God?

More more silence.

But I can taste the aftertaste of the red wine in my mouth.

Jack was real. He had to be.

Inexplicably. Strangely. Suddenly. Emboldened I feel.

Embrace the exile from your *normal* life! Jack is back, but he whispers the word *normal* as though *normal* is a most aberrant abnormality. Nin, this is your chance to live directly! Don't eat your cherry through books, movies, fantasies. Eat directly!

Jack is actually whispering from a far away place, way beyond the cochlea, the airport, the sky, the stars.

Are you for real, Jack?

Loooooooooooooooooooooong silence.

Telepathic Jack is gone. I can feel it. Gone. GONE.

chapter 13

MILK: *Water*

In New York City

i
leap into the sea
my body
an oblation to a wintry ocean
water tickles my cochlea
my armpits my toes my soles
i laugh my lungs out
but my lungs want to cough my life
back up and breathing
but in vain

o
o

o

Verrazano Bridge
stretches like a woman
far away on the horizon
kneading and wrapping and wrapping
five hundred dumplings

like what i did last evening
for my husband's casual business meeting
o
o
o

someone yells
from the bridge:
"a woman has jumped!"
must be the jogger
with a brown bandanna
i saw him just now
he had a nice smile
o
o

a pale fish
stares at
my face and flees
black green red green
injured worms
running amok
across
my face
black red green red
my face bruised
fishes look and leave

o

o

sea horses

try to untie my

knotted hair swimming

wild at zero-sum speed

over my skull into my mouth

my lips

two two-week-old

pig-blood cakes

o-shaped

speak

loud

silent

joy

o

o

o

to my right

a wise chocolate-chip starfish

bed ridden and sighing:

"another from the people world

seeking

absolute

infinite

relief

really

Buddha

I hope to stay a starfish next life."

o

o

sinking i remember

staying in the shelter

for the first time

the volunteer explained

the cycle of violence:

tension

battering

honeymoon

tension

battering

honeymoon

i thought: what honeymoon?

but

the woman next to me

nodded and broke into a misplaced chuckle:

"the sex was sooooooooooo good

afterward

it was almost worth the pain."

sinking i remember

my childhood best friend cried:

"stay,
it is your bitter fate."

o

o

o

o

sinking i remember
threatening to get a restraining order
a tiny piece of my right breast was sliced off
by his cleaver
he cried later
he cooked me dinners and gave me yellow flowers
he protected me his pregnant empress
for a week
before he threw a chair
accidentally onto my tummy
my baby fell out
blue
he cried and apologized
he cooked me dinners and gave me yellow flowers
he protected me his vacuum-womb empress
for two days
then he
accidentally
said:
"it's a girl fetus anyway."

o

o

my lips

pig-blood cakes

curve up squash into

a smile

in no time now

my baby will smile in my arms

sucking sweet warm milk

in no time now

baby and i

will be together

forever

celebrating

good water

around us

inside us

i will be

full

free

and

content

o

o

no more need

for hopes

poems
meanings
charities
hotlines
shelters
saving-faces
friends and
legal-aides
o
o

no you don't understand my dear volunteer friend
he is the king and i have no face
no mouth no eyes no ears no skin no taste buds
i am his bought special part
to say his name in bed and to heave hard
why i go back you asked
because i have no i
i have no me
i left my job
i have no money
because the chinese must not tell
beyond the four walls her family ugly
o
o

no more
his cold green eyes
his tongue

his teeth

his cigarette butts

his thing

his suits his cologne his neckties

his good husband mask

shoe horn

nose hairs

garlic fart in the air

ear grease

tooth picks

yellow booger in the sink

dandruff

ash tray

acidic burps

his Polo shirts

his flowers

his sweet words

socks that are sweaty clams

his Yankee cap

alligator belts

his beer-pizza vomits

his abused childhood pleas

his love his

promises

his body his buddies his fangs

the piece of chili on his teeth

or

was it

a red piece of my special part?

who cares now? i am free at last

o

o

o

and most of all

no more

I-protect-you-that's-why-I-tell-you-
don't-go-there-don't-do-this-don't-wear-that-
don't-speak-don't-smile-don't-look-
don't-swing-your-hair-when-you-walk-
and-please-sew-all-your-toes-up-and-I-love-you.

o

o

o

good water

sinking me

deeper

sleepier

happier

freer

my eyes

no longer red and no white

no longer thin and tight
no longer mute like
Buddha's third eye

o

o

o

i am almost back to where the milk is
death is almost complete

o

o

o

o

no longer cracked and cold
my nipples begin to shoot rivers of milk
milk rivers running wild
across my chest
rushing into my baby's throat
deeper
and deeper
warming all ten of my baby's chilly toes
pinking her ten small fingers
rivers of milk coalesce
together i and baby
bathing in a small milk sea
sea horses
starfishes
my childhood blue toy fish

sea palace sea queens sea dragon kings
my mama's house coat smells like anemones
my papa's magic pockets grow seaweed candies
my baby's mouth sucking hungrily
peacefully
amid
my best things
my blood
standing still

o

o

o

o

o

no more
my blood
standing still
alone
obediently
on the kitchen floor

o

o

I

am

free

really

my last thought

I am not thinking

as i had earlier thought

thoughts of me

a ghost coming back

picking up the ice pick

nailing his heart beats

shoe horn

prying open his mouth

packing hot chilies inside his throat

the way he packed into mine

and plucking his nose hair

clean

really

my last thought

I am inserting a nipple hot with milk

into my baby's mouth

speaking into hot baby ears

the stories of sea palace sea queens sea dragons kings

really
my last thought
I am a starfish
my papa my mama my baby
and I
together
we
starfish
and starfish
and starfish and starfish
side by side by side by side
in this way

a
circle

we

stay

till

even
after

the
earth

dies

.

chapter 14

NIN

In New York City

*O*utside the wall-size window, the Empire State Building antenna, a needle, almost pokes the skin of the morning sky as silk blue as Rob Campbell's tie. The Globalize Friday meeting is over. I have done my part—presenting my take on the Fridays spawning out there in Amsterdam, Singapore, Tokyo, Taipei, Bangkok, following the global spawning speed of one new McDonald's every five hours. My PowerPoint take is this: Market Is Saturated, Do Not Proceed on Pending Projects. Sitting at the head of the conference table, Rob is stunned solid. "What? Really, Nin? Why?"

Imagine 2060, E.D.I. Friday, now in partnership with Disney and Rupert Murdoch's News Corp., is the main attraction on the moon.

"Yes, really," I say, "stop all projects in progress." I feel an urge to stand up and declare my independence, raising my hand like Tengku Abdul Rahman did in 1957 declaring

Malaysia *merdeka* from the British ruling kings and queens, sirs and madams. But I pin down the urge; instead I say, "That's my take on the business. I'm sorry I can't stay, I need to get going, thank you, gentlemen, for listening."

But I know Rob and his kind will globalize E.D.I. Friday with or without me. It is the nature of business, they would say. Want to be nice? Stay a mom and pop store, they would say. Want to be a global giant? Be a dog-eating dog as the world of giants is a world of dogs where if you are not eating, you are eaten, that's what they would say.

Rob Campbell rises from his chair and says, "I don't think we can stop these projects now. But, go, go have fun, Nin. Go continue your FireWife photo essay and live your artistic self for five months. Really, Nin, I truly appreciate your effort to accommodate my requests, I know as a result of taking care of Friday's international sites in the past month, you could only work on your photo project part time. So go now! But stay safe, Nin." "I'll be fine," I say. Really. Rob is genuinely concerned about my safety. Street-smart Rob is a straight-shooter, a plain talker, he calls what he sees and feels. And he always wants me to be candid with him like he is candid with me. He would say, just come out and say it, tell me, Nin, tell me what you're truly thinking, speak the unspeakable, I can handle it, he would say.

I once asked Rob if I were to describe him as Wesley Snipes black, not Will Smith black, you know like Alek Wek black, not Naomi Campbell black, would he be mad? He said, hell yes! I saw on his face, he's handling *it.* But I told him I wouldn't be offended if someone describes my eyes as Margaret Cho-y and not Maggie Cheung-y because that is the fact, and the fact is that you are Wesley Snipes black, not Will Smith black. I asked why can't we understand that someone is merely describing a difference in shape or shade of color, not a difference in preference, value, beauty, standing? That's sweet and all, Rob Campbell said, but Nin, we still live in a world in constant pursuit of fairer skin, bigger eyes, larger seats, larger cars, bigger breasts, longer legs, taller men, blonder hair, bluer eyes, and of course the tallest building. I immediately thought of Malaysia's Petronas Towers and a nation's pride in owning the tallest in the world, for six years. Rob continued, therefore, if someone comments that your eyes are Margaret Cho–like not Maggie Cheung–like, Nin, you should suspect the speaker's possible bias and motive before you nod gleefully, he said, because it shouldn't matter what your eyes look like, I know what you mean, Nin, you are describing things like an open-minded, free-minded child, but these—hair, eyes, skin—are issues with long histories and politics. And I bet you Wesley Snipes and Will Smith and Alek Wek and Naomi and Margaret and Maggie, they will all be pissed to be invoked as categories for shapes of eyes, shades of skin. I know that, I said, but I thought you might have a new angle on this. Then I told Rob about my longing for a *basic* place, a place where values and preferences don't exist, only harmonious differences, only the understanding that *big* can't mean without *small*, *small* can't mean without *big*, *white* can't mean without *black*, *black* can't mean without *white*, the *strong* can't mean without the *weak*, the *prudish* can't mean without the *prurient*, a place where *good, bad, better, worse, preferred* carry no meaning. Does such a place exist? Is such a place possible? Hell no! Rob said. Hell yes, I said. I don't know where it is, but I think it exists. Rob shook his head and muttered "young people" while I imagined a utopia where differences coexist in peace.

But Telepathic Jack said utopia is by nature short-lived.

Was the prescient Jack right? Was he *real*? Jack feels like a mere dream now.

Rob Campbell is smiling. He has a handsome smile. Very Humphrey Bogart. Very Denzel. I smile back. "Thank you," I say. "And yes, in the past month I have shot no more than two rolls of film and I can't wait to shoot more, I just want you to know, I won't be reachable for five months. Ciao." There are at least fifteen E.D.I. Friday execs in the conference room. In front of these scrutinizing eyes, Rob Campbell gives me a five-seconds-too-long long hug and kiss. Full-body press. On the cheek. I feel his lips thread close to my earlobe. But today, this is the first time his giving me a cheek-kiss makes me neither wild nor wince. Inside I mean. I feel nothing.

Nothing.

It is as though my body has severed its tie with anything and everything E.D.I. Friday.

I let go of Rob.

In no time now, I'll be out of this office free. Free.

John Dartmouth, Friday's CTO, Chief Technology Officer, forty, single, a health freak, who brushes his teeth with organic milk, who sees AIDS, tsunami, influenza pandemic, famine, wars as forces of nature ameliorating quite successfully the problems of abject poverty and over-population in the world, yells out, "Nin, we'll miss you, *let's open the kimono* will have no meaning when you are not around." I see Rob Campbell frown, his huge earlobes twitch a few tics, he is handling *it*. John Dartmouth likes to use *let's open the kimono now* to start a meeting. I have heard that John likes to call meetings in his own department with his famous kimono line. But I haven't heard it firsthand until this morning, when he preempted Rob and called the meeting in his signature way while giving me a friendly smile, and here he is again uttering his prominent line, his teeth milk-white, so is his smile. I stop walking. I turn to face John Dartmouth, who is at the moment quite pleased with himself. John Dartmouth is not a man I respect. He is a man who would go to Bangkok to pin down a virgin girl half his size and think he liberates and educates her and she should thank him for his money and power. I feel a fire deep in my navel rising. I hear a voice leaping out of my mouth. My fire voice. No politeness can stop my fire tongue this time. "Well, John, now that I'm gone, you get a chance to open your own drawers instead. To jumpstart a meeting, you can say *let's open my drawers now.* And while you are ruffling inside your pants for pleasure, leisure, embers of fire, or other masturbatory info, I want you to imagine a bistro in Tokyo where girls work as tables catering to men who love to open the kimono so to speak." As I remember the *nyotaimori* girl I photographed, my fire voice turns louder. "But don't take me wrong, I would rather you speak your kimono line than just obsess about *it* in your mind. Because you say *it,* I have a chance to address *it,* like *it* or hate *it,* hone and widen your understanding about *it,* and if I don't feel like explaining *it,* I can choose to avoid *it* and avoid *you,* who think and say *it.* So, thank you for being forthright, really. And on that note, John, I shall now leave you and your drawers alone."

And I walk out.

Behind me the wrath of a bruised ego, milk-white, stands breathlessly still.

I am not afraid. Neither am I worried. I am free. Truly.

It is February 3. Friday. Almost noon.
I am standing at some street corner in Manhattan.
And I am done with E.D.I. Friday.
DONE!

But now what?

Not leaving for Bhutan until Sunday, where shall I go from here?

East? South? West? North?

I seem to have infinite options at the moment.

Standing around and savoring one's many options can't set one free. One must choose and engage. But choose how? Which way?

Listen to the undertow. Feel.

Do. Be.

Don't analyze. Don't think.

Feel the flow. Let come. Let go.

Telepathic Jack said—Don't live in books, fantasies, movies!

Live Directly!

I must not only *know* but also *live directly* who I am to be *real*ly free.

But, how many parts in "I" are there to unlock, set free?

Body? Mind? Voice?

Setting BODY free from hunger, illness, home, office, country, man-set boundaries, conventional moralities, economic constraints, and everyday routines?

Setting MIND and VOICE free from facts, norms, guilts, pieties, histories, memories, identities, worries? And fear?

Yes, fear. I fear I am not frightened enough. I fear a life

rushed and not lived, a life many layers buried, a Skin Me not frightened enough when I have long lost the Raw Me whom I can't see.

Across the street, a woman darts as though she has very little time for her to-do list. She darts just like the woman I photographed yesterday afternoon on the Verrazano Bridge. The woman, her face bruised and broken, I could hear the sound of her broken face, I saw her broken face shock even the seagulls, she looked as though she was sinking into the belly of a sea, her mouth spoke the silent sound of a broken null. I wonder where is she now.

No. Don't wonder. Don't fret. Do. Be.

But first.

To slake a quotidian hunger.

Let me buy and eat a pretzel.

As the pretzel vendor prepares my pretzel, I suddenly see that a self-imposed exile from one's regular life is a personal utopia where one can enter and exit at will.

I see a new world opening at the end of the street.

It is opening. Like a mouth.

The mouth of the new world reaches my feet when the vendor hands me my pretzel.

Almost midnight. Upper West Side. I am at the entrance to a party.

The doorman, head shaved smooth like Laurence Fishburne, purple masked, standing between a blue and a red door, explains in mandarin manner, "Red Door will propel you to a virtual world of beauty and love and pleasure, like in *The Matrix*, you get to eat a slab of the juiciest filet mignon seared just right for your taste buds, there is no getting old, no falling sick, and you get to live in what you desire as long as you like. Blue Door will bring you to the *real* world, like the world Keanu Reeves chooses in *The Matrix*, where you eat gluey porridge fighting for truth for justice saving your country your kind.

"So, which is it? Blue or red?" the doorman asks, his lips plump as plum.

"Keanu did the right thing, didn't he?" I say, self-conscious of my own lips made more naked now that I am wearing a Zorro mask.

And really, what is this, the opening of a college skit? How many times will this hired Laurence Fishburne impersonator repeat his welcoming remark this evening?

"Yes, he did," the doorman says, perfunctorily. "While Cypher did the best thing for himself."

Classic. Steak versus Porridge. The best thing versus the right thing. Cherries versus Eggs. Fire versus Water. Small Me versus Big Me.

And I ask, "Will I be denied entrance if I say the wrong door?"

"I can't say, madam," the doorman answers with tight lips, adamant like a child refusing to show the mysterious candy in his mouth.

But don't you think a mask party must be a Red Door sort of thing—a space where one is allowed to escape the prosaic temporarily, to emblazen one's latent psyche, to indulge one's secret or new self, for a change?

I wonder what is behind the blue door. A canteen serving porridge and porridge only? A wall of layered bricks? A huge poster of Mao or Keanu Reeves?

"Which is it? Red or blue? Steak or porridge?" the doorman asks again, impatience mounting in his voice.

His voice reveals a man with a quick temper. But I think, the doorman, most likely paid not much above the minimum wage, has earned the right to be impatient in a world where the richest twenty percent consumes eighty percent of the world output and resources. Or is it worse, not twenty–eighty but ten–ninety?

"Red or blue?" the doorman asks again, as though at the verge of eruption.

"Red, please."

And I choose red because Mae West says that between two evils (or two gods), one must choose the evil (or the god) one has not tried.

"Sorry, I can't hear you," the doorman says loudly. "You need to speak up!"

"Steak, give me steak!" I say.

"In that case," the doorman's stern lips blossoming into a festive smile, he too has gapped front teeth, he announces, "welcome to The Bowl of Light!" And he flings open the red door.

A tsunami, gargantuan in volume and intensity, of music and heat and light washes over the whole of me—face, body, every inch of skin, flesh, every hollow in my bone marrow. Sucked in, transported, lost, I stare at the light consisting of thousands of strobe-like lightbulbs on the walls made pink and dimmed by a torrential cascade of bordello-pink glass bottles, glass beads, fuchsia glass witch balls hung from where the ceiling meets the walls. Disoriented, I feel a shortness of breath pressed shorter in light of light, I inhale deeper to lock in a huge lungful of oxygen. The air smells of fresh lilies, sweat, cake, cherries, perfume, meat, and a lingering spicy fishy twist. And the place is smaller than I expected, cramped with a group of masked men and women swaying their bodies like tree gods going amok.

To my left I see a woman, bare back, clad in a skimpy black dress, slithering her body against the wall at the end of a narrow reddish hallway, her hair tar-black, the tips of her ten fingers swollen red and big as cherries, she moves as though a lizard slithering to her own beat. As my eyes become better adjusted to the world of red, I see that she is slithering to pin something against the wall; the something is a masked man, about her height, beginning to swallow, one by one, the cherries gloving the tips of her fingers. He ingests the last cherry. He leaves her behind. He walks toward the foyer and me.

He yells HELLO BEAUTIFUL and asks loudly, slowly, clearly, near my ear (his breath cherry sweet), if I want to be publicly cherried or privately cherried, as though the ten cherries he just ate were ample only to fill a small nook in his tummy. I reply at the top of my lungs, I have no desire to be cherried at all, and I articulate each word valiantly as though the question was whether I like to be publicly or privately raped. Why not, he asks. I have no idea what "cherried" means, I say, strongly, calmly, leaving no room for mistake, but my voice hoarse, from a throat straining to shout beyond its means. Publicly cherried is what you just saw, he yells over the music, the white of his tux gleaming in pink, privately cherried is what you just saw carried out in the privacy of a room, no less no more, his eyes naughty. I see, I say. Can one cherry someone else in lieu of being cherried herself? I inquire, feigning a worldly woman at the pinnacle of her charm and power confidently surveying her prey and insinuating what she desires. Sure, as you desire, he says. But the loss of interest in his voice is obvious—he must be an eater, not an eatee. But first, let's dance, he suggests. I say I just arrived, I think I'd like to stand around for a bit longer. He smiles, shrugs, and walks away. At the end of the hallway, the lizard woman is now nowhere to be found, she must have entered a nearby room or lounge. For a moment, I believe the lizard woman to be the cat-eyed, tar-haired foot reflexologist who gave me a most awakening massage just this afternoon—she who said her massage will make my feet fit for exile, she who gave me the invitation to this mask party with "the possibility of an orgy."

I am not ready for cherries, let alone an orgy.

I came to *see* an orgy, not *be* an orgist.

I turn to my right, a masked server, goateed, gives me a brimming smile holding a platter mottled with shrimp balls and calamari rings. The calamari rings look just like p.s. squid, short for peppered and salted squid. In college, Lara would order two, sometimes three, large take-out orders of p.s. squid from Ming Garden behind CVS on Main Street and she would eat them like Cape Cod chips while cramming through the night during midterms and finals. Lara named her cancer pain p.s. squid. She said now that she has the advanced stage of cancer she gets to eat p.s. squid every second of the day. She said sometimes she swallows them without chewing. But sometimes she eats p.s. squid with a sip of tangerine juice and that gives p.s. squid a tangy flavor. She said hers is the best way of managing pain, eating pain like it's your favorite finger food, swallow and it's gone, swallow and it's gone. Lara died in pain. Excruciating pain. The goateed waiter asks if I want some calamari. I say, later.

I notice, behind the bartender who has just handed me a fluted snifter of cognac, an inconspicuous balcony door is waiting, waiting to be parted, entered, known. I quickly squeeze behind the bartender to open the door to the balcony. Fresh air is what I need.

Outside, the night is thick with uncommonly warm February air; I feel relieved. Seeping through the balcony door, the music is a muffled roar. At the foot of the building, Central Park looms dark and wide, like an orifice waiting to be studied. I feel a sudden tightening of skin at the base of my spine, the tightening reminds me of the time I spent in the office of my political science professor in college. I was so young then, not even eighteen. I went to his weekly office hour weekly, just so I could be alone with him for some precious, pathetic, stomach-wrenching five minutes, asking him in sentences far from coherent about various political theories and their applicability, but in truth, all those times, I couldn't help but stare in giddy tenderness at the soft shape of his mouth, I wanted so bad to say *kiss me now.* But of course, nothing was said. So nothing happened. Only the skin at the base of my spine got tighter and tighter as his lips moved to shape more and more scholarly-sounding words falling on my ears like bubbles softly drying and sucking on skin. But I knew, had I said *kiss me now,* the sky would have collapsed, and I would have been too powerless to turn it into a soft-landing blanket or a tiger with wings, and the sky would have crushed me flat like a piece of humiliated raw tuna fish bruised and unwanted and naked on a white porcelain plate. Lara advised that I should just say nothing, stand up, close the door, and sit on him, leaving him no time to think. I said nothing. And I sat on nothing. I am sure he has *not* a morsel of memory of the awkward me now, but Lara, I am sure, he remembers. He must. He pressed his lips tighter whenever Lara appeared in his field of vision. I noticed these things because in college where there was Lara, there was I.

Lara said, Nin, what are you waiting for? Bad health? Old age? Be who you are! Now! Not who you should be. Fly.

Fly immensely. She said.

Eat.

Love wide.

Live full.

Live a full life! She said.

I thought, what does a *full life* look like? But I didn't ask.

Instead I said, let me stay, let me take care of you, Lara, I'll take a leave from my job and take care of you, I know Mahar, he won't mind.

Lara said no. Don't get me wrong, Nin, I *do* want you to quit your job, but that stems from my anti-globalization stance, quit your job and do what you like, not here wasting your life seeing me die, she said, we are saying our final goodbye now, I am not afraid, Nin, I know I'll be back as I am again, maybe not as polyandrous as I have been but close, you know. She smiled her mischievous smile. You can call it Buddhism or Hinduism or Zen, whatever it is, I know I am not done with my life, I can still feel so much love, I'll be back, Nin, I have faith in returning as I am in next life, I have so much love left, I believe in love, in desiring to love and be loved, touch and be touched, and I believe in next life, in next next life, and next next next life. She paused. A long pause. Then she said, even if I can't come back, I know my love and spirit will live on. I know, she said.

Lara died last fall.

"Where are you now, Lara?" I probe the soft wind drifting about the balcony.

"Can you hear me?"

I see the soft wind nodding ... nodding ...

"I'm ready to fly immensely," I whisper to the wind and the sky. "Can you hear me?" I whisper to the dark orifice.

"The stripes."

Shocked. I turn around. A man is standing at the far corner of the balcony. How long has he been standing there? He's walking toward me.

"The stripes on your stockings look like nectar guides on the lip of an orchid," he says.

What?

But I feel the nose of his words sniffing under my skirt.

The profound power of ripened words spoken at ripened moments.

He is standing in front of me now. The shape of his mouth. I gasp. Our eyes meet. He quivers. I too tremble, for I just realize I've known him since flat worms first learned how to penis-fence to decide the burden of motherhood in the beginning of time. That's how long I've known him and been deprived of and looking for him. Since the beginning.

Who is he? you ask.

He is Ardor. Passionate. Full. Baggage-free.

Free from the burden of food, law, shelter, decency, safety, ego, history, future.

Free from a body leaden with birth, life, guilt, age, illness, death.

He embodies the ideal essence of a single moment of love free from time. Impermanent. Anomalous. Disconnected.

He is the single-pointed purest peak without the baggage of ascents and descents.

He is the object of my desire my quest.

"I love the shape of your lips," he says.

How did it begin? It. This. He in his black mask and I in my beet-red Zorro mask standing a foot apart, faceless, nameless, naked, chest to chest in this small and plush powder room made illusorily large by its wall-size mirrors, and we not touching except for his Man occasionally touches my navel and he would let go of a soft moan and open his mouth a slight sliver wider and I would feel the surge of a numbing fire in my lips ready to eat cherries turned tight and puce and big as plums.

How did it begin? It. This.

I love the wing-tipped upper lip of his mouth. That's how one.

And he is the object of my quest. That's how two.

And I am hungry and ready to eat a feast of pleasure. That's how three.

And I cease curbing myself. That's how four.

As I move down to his stomach, his hot and musky skin turns muskier, and I think of how my stop curbing myself means my start lying to Mahar, and I hear an inner voice whispering in my ears: Some cherries are like fish, some are sweet, some are muskier than the abdominal sac of a male musk deer, don't think, be yourself, eat. Still behind the whispering inner voice is a fading voice screaming a silent scream: You mustn't eat illicit cherries, they can damage the organ we call trust, they can make your lips itch, for life they'll itch.

To eat or not to eat?

But he is the catalyst. He can let out the original me. He is the utopia I seek.

Eat.

life

Know and let fly your fire, but always always always
maintain and nurture your water . . .
Listen to your skin,
let it breathe, let it feast, let it be the catalyst . . .
THE MYTH

chapter 15

Nin: *Vessel*

*E*at. Eating. A trembling cherry. Or is it a trembling plum?

I am eating a trembling world in the shape of a bowl.

The more I eat, the more the fruit speaks of other things.

The world as I once knew is ending, the world as I never knew beginning.

No, Jack says, everything will go back to normal in five months.

Will it?

Eat. *Real* sexual liberties will bring forth other liberties. A voice speaks.

A sinking woman abreast with rivers of milk tries to stop me from eating, she says: I am Water, Nin, don't eat, look at your past, go back, back to where the milk is.

Comes the young Taipei woman who leases her forehead as ad space, she says: I am Water, don't eat cherries, cherries carry only empty calories, drink a bowl of egg flower soup instead!

I stop eating.

But the Bangkok girl astride the back of a fly wants to play with me, she yells through the wind: I am Fire, come with me, let's play, let's eat, your earlobes will give you the guiltless freedom you want, eat, eat, you will set us all free if you eat!

I eat.

Comes the sushi-table woman offering me some sashimi, I say no, she says: I am Water, stay still and be dormant, don't eat, don't open your nose, it will bring you the wrath of meat.

I hesitate.

Comes the Amsterdam woman who gawks at her cup of coffee, her agitated thumb rubbing her left nipple, she tells me: I am Water, plums and cherries will make your hands your lips itch, for life they'll itch, don't touch, don't eat.

I stop eating.

But Wing, the beautiful woman in Singapore, pushes the gawking woman off and speaks, forcefully: I am Fire, listen to your skin, Nin, let it breathe, let it feast, let it give you the births you need, make bare your feet, the tempo of love is suck and savor, suck and savor, you will set all women free if you eat! Eat!

I kiss and eat. Harder.

I am close to ecstasy, touching gently the cherry skin, its belly, its every whisper, every word, every breath.

Then, I hear them speak, in one voice they speak:

We are two fires four waters. Water leads. Together we will impart this mantra and only this. Between grounded guilts and pieties, fly. Between eggs, you may eat a cherry. But, always love. Love widely. Widely. Always nurture your base, your egg, the water from which all lives begin, the mother from which you learn and take, the land from which you leap into flight, the order from which chaos derives its meaning. Know and let fly the tongues of your fire your sky your yang, but always always always maintain and nurture your water your earth your yin. Always nurture and respect the still, the empty, the inside, the descent, the silent, the background, the sleeping—the yin in your being/having/doing. Always breathe evenly and mindfully. Breathe. Evenly. Evenly.

Ecstasy evens out a bit.

But the girl in a flaming orange sari named Lakshmi stops me from cooling, her power, her magic, her heat spreading from inside my navel and heaving in between my thighs. She says she is Lakshmi, once known as Fire, now a girl, a wife, a tiger, killed in a fire. She says, eat, eat, sexual liberty is the catalyst. Catalyst! Fire is becoming fuller and hotter. Fire is sexing every inch of my skin. Sexing. Sexing. I'm kissing her brows, her nose-ringed nose, her nutmeg-scented mouth, her breasts, her navel the shape of a tiny bowl, her skin muskier than a musk deer. She is parting and eating my rose. Rose. Now. Wow. New Skin touching. New Eyes seeing. New Mouth breathing, eating. Eating. Vessel afire. Four parts fire.

New Me is here.

I see now I have fire wings.

Fire wings can galvanize other hidden or sodden wings.

I see now even the Water Women can have fire wings.

I see now female freedom can start only with her body freeing. Fleeing. Flying.

Tongues of fire flying.

F l y i n g.

Just before sharp bliss, at the corner of my Fire Tiger eye, I see Mian, my small sister, remember her, she is not choking in tapioca mud as she has always been in my mind's eye, she is smiling eyebrow to eyebrow in her next life, she says: It's not your fault, Jie, it's not your fault. A tear glides down my cheek.

I see now this will not be the first time I embark on a Temporary Exile from Regular Life. I see now, only in exile I am a woman of my own kingdom. A queen. This is my truth. My myth. Unsponsored. An island. Disconnected from regular facts and theories and baggage and duty. A place of imperishable freedom. Imperishable bliss.

I see now, only in exile, I have fire wings.

An old ecstasy, breathing a desire as old as air fire earth

water, bursts open like a ripest mango dislodging memories of sweet eating of desires in the beginning of beginning.

Not a Can Be.

Not a May Be.

I simply Am.

I Am. At the moment of ecstasy.

My journey begins here. Spiritually. Physically.

Join me.

chapter 16

LAKSHMI: *Fire*

$\mathcal{I}$t is raining lions and tigers outside. I know Water is slamming her biggest lion and tiger rain onto Earth to prevent my birth. But I am not afraid. I have a heartbeat as ancient and fetal as Time. I am Fire. I have a four parts fire seed between my eyes. I am Lakshmi, Parvati. I mean, I was Lakshmi, daughter of Sita. I have finished planting stories of women I met in my journey in your mind's eye. I am ready for my birth. I want to partake in life. Life. Now. Again. Not as a tree. Not as a starfish. But as a girl. As your child. I am here to plant my jade seed in your navel. Will you be my mama, Parvati?

Yes, Lakshmi. Come. Come. Parvati sits up. She is panting from seeing ten thousand miles of dreams. She saw the white elephant with wings again in her dream, the winged white elephant has forty-four pure gold nose rings. Parvati suddenly feels this urge to go to Varanasi, bathe in Ganges, and touch trees. A small fire begins to simmer, urging her, driving her happy, dizzy, hungry. Driving her to long for his fullness inside her. Again. She leans over to her husband, Chen, and touches him. Moments later, Parvati closes her eyes and shakes as Chen shoots his silver snakes.

Lakshmi quivers and enters into her next life.

A fire.

A tiger.

A love.

An echoing voice guides her heartbeat. The voice hums:

When you break a fruit of a banyan tree you see very tiny seeds and when you break a seed you see nothing in it and what you do not see is the essence of the banyan tree.

Listen to your skin. Let it breathe. Let it eat. Let it be the catalyst. Let it give you the births you need.

Four parts fire. Breathe.

Sleep like Fire. Breathe.

Walk like Fire. Fly like Fire.

Eat like Fire. EatFire. Eat. Eat.

EatFire EatFire EatFire. EatEatEat.

Breathe. EatFire. EatFire. Breathe. Eat.

EatFire EatFire EatFire EatFire EatFire Eat.

EatFire EatFire EatFire EatFire EatFire Breathe . . .

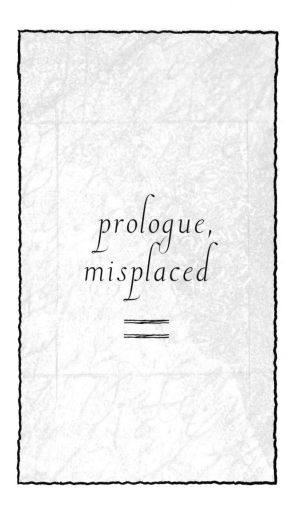

prologue,
misplaced

$\mathcal{T}$here are plenty of beliefs as to what happened in the beginning of time. This is what actually took place:

It all began with an egg. Not golden as many have assumed but black as milk. Yes, you heard it right. Milk then was black as squid ink is now. How milk later became white as rice is another story for another time, for the politics of which alone can run countless shuhu and thus countless of pages. (Shuhu, if you haven't already heard, is a unit of time, more or less eighteen thousand years.) Back to the egg. Inside the egg was a sac of black milk in the state of hundun—primordial chaos. Inside the sac of black milk was a sleeping woman—not man as many historians now maintain. She was nameless at first. Later, some astronomer-slash-adviser to the Emperor-slash-author of the Book of Time named her Nuwa.

In her sleep, Nuwa dreamed. Nuwa often dreamed dreams the size of the egg. When Nuwa dreamed, the egg hummed the beat of the dream: Hum. HumHum. Hum. HumHum. Hum. Once Nuwa had a dream larger than the egg itself. The egg hummed without breaks: HUMHUM HUMHUMHUMHUMHUMHUMHUMHUMHUM. Because the egg hummed without rest, structural fatigue, as you call it today, occurred. The egg broke. Nuwa awoke. Exactly when the egg broke, I can't tell you for sure, for I am lousy at math and in general suspicious of precise dates and facts. How humans later became super (a modern term) obsessed with precision and perfection and flawless determinacy and single-pointed truth is, again, a story for another time.

Back to when the egg broke: Nuwa awoke. Nuwa stood up, pushing away two halves of egg. The top half became the sky, stars, sun, air, fire. The bottom half turned into the ground, plants, animals, gemstones, earth, water. This newly created world was permeated with the sweet smell of milk because the omnipresent Water, though clear in color, tasted like milk then. The milky taste of water reminded Nuwa of the sac in the egg in which she had slept since the genesis of genesis. As you may have surmised, Nuwa stayed and played in Water all the time. She gave the oceans the endearing nickname of Milk Oceans, the rivers Milk Rivers, the lakes Milk Lakes. In a nutshell, Nuwa hung out in Water so long that she ultimately completely lost her gift of flying without knowing what was lost and what flying was like.

Indeed for many shuhu after the world began, Nuwa swam in Water eating sea cocoa mint and playing with sea dragonflies and starfishes and sea zebras.

By the way, you may have imagined a Nuwa standing Venus-like on an open giant shell. Nuwa was not Venus-esque. By the present Eurocentric standard, Nuwa was far from gorgeous. But in her time, namely the beginning of time, there was neither the value of ugly nor the idea of beauty. In her time, a mottled brown hen was merely different from a yellow kingfisher or a vermilion peacock. And the language spoken then was a language unconstrained by the articles *a* or *an* or *the*, or singulars or plurals, or specific tenses. It was a language ignorant of good, bad, evil, worse, worst, better, best, super best, and super super best.

One day, however, Nuwa spotted a tiger with wings soaring and plummeting gyre-like in the sky.

Nuwa had never seen tigers fly before.

Intrigued, Nuwa asked, "Can you teach me how to fly?"

The tiger replied, "Sure, but first, you need to get yourself a pair of wings and only Fire knows how to make wings for flying."

Nuwa was about to ask more about Fire and wings when Water interrupted in an apprehensive voice. "Stop! You mustn't go to Fire!"

"Why mustn't I?" Nuwa asked.

Water struggled to explain. "Because . . . Fire . . . is . . . is . . . Bad."

"What is Bad?"

"Bad is . . . is . . . NotGood."

"What is NotGood?" Nuwa was confused indeed.

"NotGood . . . can . . . can make you die!" Water replied.

Long story short. Nuwa wanted her wings. Water said no, and in the name of love and protection, leg-shackled Nuwa to a giant banyan tree at the yellow muddy shore of the longest Milk River. Needless to say, Fire was angry at Water. No. Let me rephrase. Fire was furious. Hence began the longest, fiercest, most cacophonous of battles—the battle between Fire and Water.

Meanwhile, Nuwa wanted to flee. She wanted Bad. She wanted NotGood. She wanted wings. She wanted to fly like the tiger with fire wings. But she was manacled with shackles made of the shell of a golden cooter. Impossible manacles!

Numerous shuhu went by, the battle between Fire and Water continued. One night, in the infinitesimal light of stars, Fire swung a fireball at Water but missed, and the fireball hit the southwestern corner of the sky and broke a mammoth hole in it, a gargantuan explosion erupted, and five seeds of four parts fire fell from the fiery hole in the sky into Nuwa's palm. Five seeds! Nuwa looked up and garnered an idea. She took a handful of yellow mud and kneaded it into a bowl. She whispered into the belly of the bowl the shape and essence of what she wanted, such as a pair of fire wings, flying beyond the stars and the sky, hands touching the furry armpits of clouds, nibbling on a plum until its juice was squandered, sucking a ripest mango, smelling a skin muskier than the musk deer, eating a cherry turned puce and tight.

For many days and nights, Nuwa spoke into the belly of this tiny bowl. She spoke slowly and surely about the spirits of all, and I mean *all*, objects of her desire. She named each of the objects Ardor. When she was finally done, she put a seed of four parts fire into the belly of the bowl and named the bowl Utopia and sealed the mouth of the bowl with a ball of yellow mud and threw it through the hole in the sky onto the other side of earth.

Looking at the bowl vanishing into the hole, Nuwa knew she had forgotten to bestow upon the bowl its destiny. And she worried that the mouth of the bowl might have been sealed too tightly. Little did she know, the bowl went on to bring not only the beginning of imagination and quest but also the start of pleasure and pain, sorrow and joy, loss and gain.

Concerned about the incompetence of the bowl Utopia, Nuwa garnered another idea and took another handful of yellow mud and began molding a yellow mud doll. And then another. She made four mud women in all. She gave each of them one seed of four parts fire.

The first mud doll Nuwa made, she made after her own image. She named her Vessel, short for the Vessel of Desire, and inserted the seed of four parts fire in between Vessel's legs and gave the seed the fate of craving the touch of blissful flight.

Her second mud doll, Nuwa formed her after her imagined image of Fire—a girl with the eyes of the winged fire tiger. She named her Fire, short for Fire Seed of Desire, and planted a flaming seed between her eyes, and conferred on her the most intense force of freedom and ardor, and bestowed upon her the destiny and torque to fan hot the seed in between Vessel's legs.

The third mud doll Nuwa made, she made different from her own image. She named her Innocent, short for the Innocence before Freedom was Curbed. Innocent had the might to feed Vessel's mind with boundless freedom. Innocent's spirit too was four parts fire.

Nuwa made the fourth mud doll after her own image and named her Mirror, short for the Mirror of Vessel's Life and Desire, and granted Mirror the magical fate to mimic Vessel's shape of life if Vessel were to act on and live her fire desire. Mirror was also four parts fire. But only Mirror and Vessel were made after Nuwa's own image.

Then Nuwa blessed Vessel with the destiny of meeting Fire, Innocent, and Mirror in each of Vessel's lifetimes to come, as long as Time lives. Then she threw them through the orifice in the sky to the other side of earth.

Afterward, Nuwa mended the sky and lay down upon the earth and died.

Stunned, Water made four mud women of her own, all after her own image, and, in the name of love and protection, named them: Egg, Stable, Mother, and Water, and fated each of them the life of four parts water, and granted each of them in each of Vessel's lifetimes the chance to meet and steer Vessel back to safety and stability and posterity.

Then Water threw the mud women through the hole in the sky so as to land them on the other side of earth.

Then, in the name of posterity, Water made a man and named him Man and gave him seeds to spend and sent him after these women through the hole in the sky.

Such was the beginning of mankind.

In the largest scheme of things
This is the tale of eight women
Bonded since the beginning of time
Despite fragmentation and displacement in our time
Their stories intertwine
Over the Body and Mind of Time
Organically yet not too organically
Accidentally yet not too accidentally
Bind
Unbind
Bind
Unbind

Acknowledgments

Without Sandy Dijkstra, my agent extraordinaire, I would still be writing in my closet. Without Lorna Owen, my immensely gifted editor and more, *FireWife* would be dimmer and worse. Without Nan Talese, my publisher, *FireWife* would be in a shelter, not a home.

I thank Robert Stone for sharing his wisdom. I thank Amy Blackstone for saying, *Let go of your editorial self and be free.* I thank Laura King for encouragement.

Deep thanks to Elise Capron, Taryn Fagerness, and Elisabeth James for comments, humor, intelligence, and support.

Without the Wellesley College Mary Elvira Stevens Traveling Fellowship, *FireWife* would be a different story and I a different person. I thank my alma mater for this and much more. In Bangkok, I thank Kanit Suriyasat for offering me a room in her exquisite teak house to write and rest. In Paris, I thank Natalie Thiriez for letting me stay in her apartment when I knew no one. I thank Mr. Yee Thiam Sun for connecting me with UNESCO officers in Seoul, Bangkok, and Phnom Penh. My huge gratitude also goes to my dean and professors at Yale University for a year of absence to complete *FireWife*.

Many friends commented on *FireWife* in her various incarnations, in part or whole, over the years. My sincere thank-you to ALL of you. For painstakingly helping me see a better *FireWife*, I especially thank Alexandra Rose Wagner, Anita Brosen, Ann Brandon, Anna Kaye Ling, Arati Tripathi, Bingyi Huang, Dan Fine, Franz Zerrudo, Iona Rozeal Brown, Janet Chen, Jennifer Feeley, Jo Grissom, Livia Yang, Lynne Gately, Mei Chin, Meredith Golomb, Peg Meyers, Rei Matsushita, Rosyln Chao, Sarah Silbert, Sindy Yeh, Sue-Yi Wang, and Yuki Asakura.

Finally and immeasurably, love to Gwen-Zoe, Ma, Pa, Aun, Shyue, Kai, and Tseming. For loving me enough to let me go and be. For being there. For shoulders. For ears. For love. For life. For a bond like the bonds between air and lungs, fish and water, banyan and banyan.

A Note About the Author

Born and raised in Malaysia, Tinling Choong received a B.A. from Wellesley College and is working toward her Ph.D. in East Asian Languages and Literatures at Yale University. *FireWife* is her publishing debut. She is at work on her new novel.

A Note About the Type

The text of this book was set in a digital version of Centaur. Centaur was created in 1914 for the Metropolitan Museum by the noted type and book designer Bruce Rogers (1870–1957). The cut of the letters is based on Venetian old-style typefaces by the fifteenth-century printer Nicolas Jenson. Centaur has a beauty of line and proportion that has been widely acclaimed since its release.

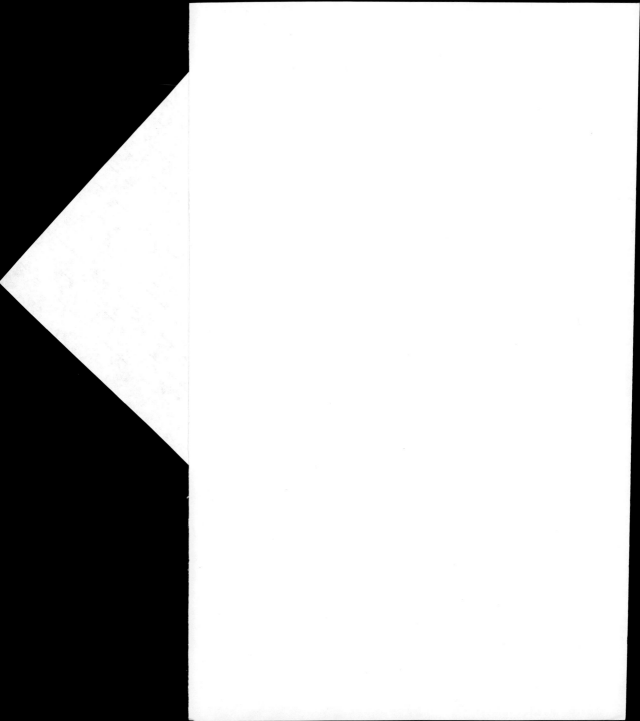

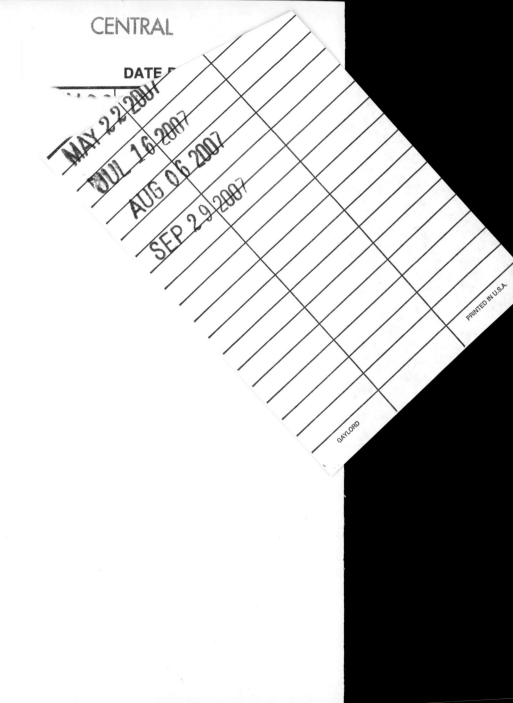